MURDER IN RETROGRADE

GREG HICKEY

Murder in Retrograde

Copyright © 2025 by Greg Hickey

Paperback ISBN: 978-1-7330937-5-0
Ebook ISBN: 978-1-7330937-6-7

We got to have you. We got to have sharpers with private licenses hiding information and dodging around corners and stirring up dust for us to breathe in.

— Raymond Chandler, *The Little Sister*

ONE

Ellory Schuyler lived in the wreckage of a spaceship that had crash-landed in the middle of what used to be Topanga State Park. At least that's what it looked like. It was a clear, tepid April morning with a few wisps of clouds and a hard climbing sun that promised the real heat was yet to come. I had taken an early airtran out of Chicago and switched lines in Denver before alighting at the Central Los Angeles Depot just over an hour after I walked out my front door. By the time my rental car rounded the last bend of the private road snaking into the Santa Monica Mountains and Schuyler's home materialized behind some transplanted oak trees, I would have killed for a second cup of coffee.

The remaining park leading up to Schuyler's house was mostly dead land: pale, sun-scorched stone dotted with patches of yucca and chaparral. It was clear the seasonal fires had scoured this place many times over. I had already seen a few scattered blazes on my approach to LA. But the winding road to Schuyler's house was guarded by those well-placed oak groves, the same trees I had seen lining the Brentwood and Palisades streets below. I supposed they were native plants, but they looked distinctly out of place here atop a mountain of wasted rock. They were effective though. I hadn't spotted Schuyler's house until I was right on top of it.

From my approach, the visible structure appeared to be a modest, one-story home with sparse windows and an undulating roof. At nighttime, one might almost mistake the thing for part of the mountain. But in the daylight, the dull charcoal sheen of hydro- and solar cells was apparent. I left the car with a ruddy-faced chauffeur and walked to the side of the house. Beyond the single level visible from the driveway, the mansion continued down the slope of the mountain, sprawling along the curves of the rock. From this angle, I could see the back of the top floor was a floor-to-ceiling window, and I guessed the same was true of the stories below me. I counted seven levels, each wider than the one above it. Where there were no cells, glass skylights studded the sinuous roof. Below the house, there was nothing but kilometers of mountain and forest leading down to the seemingly tiny houses of the Palisades. It looked like an awful lot of money to spend on a heap of metal and glass strewn against the rock face. I figured Schuyler couldn't decide between a downtown skyscraper penthouse or a secluded mountain retreat and settled on both. I guess when you're worth a hundred billion dollars, you can have your cake and eat it too.

As I returned to the front of the house, I did a mental run-through of the brief my web scraper had compiled from its search. Ellory Schuyler: founder and CEO of Schuyler Space Industries. Engineering degree from the University of Texas. Designed the rocket that made the first successful manned mission to Mars. One son, William, one daughter, Vera. Neither involved with their father's business. Wife, Isabel, of over thirty years, deceased thirteen months ago. Pancreatic cancer. Estimated net worth: the aforementioned $102 billion. I didn't know why he wanted to hire a private detective. The message he'd sent me didn't say. But it was obvious he could pay, and I badly needed the money.

The butler was waiting for me at the front. Another human servant. I didn't think anyone had those anymore, although the bio-plastic-faced man before me was doing his best robot impersonation.

"Welcome, Mr. Carver," he said. "Please come in."

He stiffly held open a door I hadn't noticed when I drove up, and

I stepped inside.

Somehow, the California sunlight seemed brighter inside the house than out. Straight ahead, the full-length window I had observed earlier looked out over the rest of the house and the coastline below. To the right, a stairway wound down to the next level, accompanied by the white rail of a stairlift. Other than the distant horizon, there were no straight lines in sight. The ceiling arched three meters above my head. The walls curved gently outward to maximize the concave window and the incredible view. Anywhere in the room the southern sun couldn't reach from the window, there was a skylight above to provide ample illumination.

"Mr. Schuyler will be with you in a moment," the butler said. "May I offer you anything?"

"Coffee," I said. "Black."

He tapped the screen on his forearm and led me into the expansive sitting room. The furniture looked as though the movers had hauled it in, set it down and forgot to arrange it. The pieces were as cold and solid as museum sculptures. I had heard of this design but hadn't witnessed it up close. I sank into a reclining armchair on the left side of the room and put my feet on the matching ottoman. What looked like finely worked marble conformed to my body so that it felt like I was floating on clouds. It was better than advertised. But I wasn't here to sit around. Besides, I had a chair at home that did the same thing after I broke it in over the past decade. I pushed myself to my feet. A long glass coffee table extended diagonally past the chair, too far away to set a drink on while seated. On the opposite side of the table, a second armchair and ottoman faced the center of the room. In a corner under a skylight, there was a round half loveseat. A chaise longue ran parallel to the window on the far side of the room. The only organization to the space I could see was that the furniture framed a direct path from the front door to the window. I took it.

I stood at the glass and decided I could get used to living in a place like this. It wasn't much to look at from the outside, but from where

I stood now, with the distant houses below inconsequential blots dwarfed by the cobalt ocean and the cornflower sky, the advantages were clear.

When I turned around, the butler was there, a steaming cup of coffee in his hand.

"Thanks," I said, "Mr. ..."

"Cherrier, sir. Renley Cherrier."

I nodded and sipped the coffee. It was hot and strong enough to dissolve graphene. Perfect.

Most of the right wall of the room was filled by a screen displaying a Martian landscape: barren copper soil, craggy umber mountains, hazy amber sky. A harsh wind scattered dust and loose tawny pebbles across the desolate expanse. I suspected an artificial video, though I wouldn't have put it past Schuyler to have a livecast from our neighboring planet. On the opposite wall, there was a painting of the kind you didn't see anymore outside of galleries and museums. It looked like oil on canvas and depicted a young man on a sailboat, surrounded by green waves with a shadow of land in the distance. The boat appeared strong and sleek, capable of traversing any body of water under the boy's firm hand. He must have been about thirteen, his wavy hair so blond it was almost white, his cool green eyes fixed on the actual ocean beyond the sitting room window.

"That boat was the first thing Mr. Schuyler ever designed." Cherrier lifted his chin toward the painting. "He was twelve years old. He built it in a year and sailed it to the Cocos Islands by himself when he was sixteen."

"Sailed from where?" I asked.

"Beaumont, Texas. Evidently, he said the Cocos Islands were as far away as you could go before you had to come back."

Not as far as outer space, I thought.

Together, we looked at the painting and watched each other out of the corners of our eyes. It was clear Cherrier's affection ran deeper than professional loyalty. He was proud of his employer, almost like a father to a son. Aside from that, he was entirely unremarkable. Average height and build, a face you wouldn't remember if it was sticking you up in broad daylight. He was ideally suited to his position. If I spent more than a day or two in this house, I wouldn't even notice him taking care of me. My coat would be removed from my shoulders and stowed away, a drink would be placed at my side, but I would never fully recall someone having done those things. In that way, he was like the old, gnarled oaks that shielded this house from the roads below. They did their job exceedingly well, but once you got beyond them and saw the dull metal lump of a building with the ocean in the distance, the oaks were easy to forget.

"It seems a long way from sailboats to rockets," I said.

"Quite, sir," Cherrier said. "But I suppose Mr. Schuyler never believed that." He glanced at his screen. "Mr. Schuyler will see you now. My apologies for the delay."

I followed Cherrier out of the sitting room, around the corner and down the flight of stairs that curved along the side of the house. We stopped two floors down, and Cherrier led me past another windowed wall to what looked like a dead end. He gave two crisp knocks, and a door slid noiselessly open in front of us. I entered.

TWO

My first impression of Ellory Schuyler was that he was incredibly vain or a bit self-deluded. Maybe both. His holohead had a tall, slender face, a strong chin, high, sculpted cheekbones and a narrow, slightly hooked nose, with thick hair as white as sun-bleached bone, and green eyes that could twinkle like emeralds or cut like a jealous lover. I had seen a lot of good holoheads, but his was the best. The holographic projection clung to his actual face even when he made a sharp movement, and there didn't seem to be any lag between his actual and projected expressions. It was probably good enough to flummox a retscan. The problem was, it didn't match his body. His figure was heavy, ponderous, shapeless. His digital face made him look like he was a former athlete who still swam laps every morning, but his body barely seemed to have enough energy to lift him out of his chair. He wore a tailored suit that did him no favors and a pair of thin black gloves—perhaps to convince himself he might actually work with paper and ink.

He was seated behind a desk of zigzagging, fine gray stone that somehow counterbalanced into a stable platform. The walls behind him and to his right were each covered by a white screen where I guessed he did his design work—assuming he still did his own work. Two screens on the wall to his left transitioned through a series of engineering schematics, either to provide inspiration or to showcase his past efforts. Near that wall, there was a low, light gray, kidney-shaped couch in what looked like velvet and a long, dark gray, additive wood coffee table. The door I entered through was in the front-right corner of the room, giving Schuyler a commanding view of the floor-to-ceiling window and the ocean below.

"Welcome, Mr. Carver. Thank you for coming." He indicated a gray bioleather chair on the window side of the desk. It wasn't as comfortable as the form-fitting one in his sitting room, but I made do.

He nodded at the cup in my hand. "Would you like some more coffee? Something stronger?"

I declined.

"It's Marcus, isn't it?" he said.

"Yes."

"As in Aurelius?"

"As in Garvey," I said. "And my grandfather."

"Was he a private investigator too?"

"A police officer."

"And your father?"

"A lawyer. Public defender."

"I understand you were once a police officer." Schuyler bit his words off like a morsel of seared foie gras.

"I was."

"But not anymore."

His twinkling eyes locked on mine. The wrinkles around the right side of his mouth dimpled as his lips parted slightly. His eyes were smiling. His mouth was not. I waited for him to ask. But he let his eyes go on shining for another five seconds and said nothing.

"I understand you have a job for me," I said.

Schuyler spread his gloved hands on the surface of his desk. "I got your name from another lawyer," he said. "Private defense attorney. A friend of a friend, in Chicago. Nathan Hines, I think it was."

"Hayes," I said. "An old friend of my father's. I did some work for him once."

Schuyler stood and walked around me to the window. I waited as he stayed there, looking out on the glimmering California coastline below.

"So a cop and a public defender," he said without turning around. "I bet your granddad didn't like that."

I could hear the crackle of time burning through my dried-out account. Schuyler wasn't paying me to sit here discussing my parentage. I got up and leaned against his desk, facing Schuyler's back, and wondered how he would react if the furniture collapsed under my weight. I said, "They had their differences. Every family does. But when it came down to it, they both understood they were working for the same thing."

Schuyler looked over his shoulder and raised one silver eyebrow. "Which was?"

"What the taxpayers paid them to do: keep innocent people safe."

Schuyler nodded slowly, approvingly. "Men of principle." He turned to face me. "I hope that you're of the same stock, Mr. Carver. That's why I asked you to come here." He stood with his legs spread wide and hands on his hips, blocking the window with his substantial frame. "I'd like to believe that I'm a man of principle. That I've done things the right way. That I haven't taken any shortcuts or hurt people unnecessarily. I hope to leave this world a better place than I found it. But not everyone shares my convictions."

He returned to his chair and slumped into it. The right side of his mouth parted to reveal bright, predatory, white teeth. I noticed he never smiled fully, but only in these half-grins somewhere between a chuckle and a leer. It didn't do much to convince me we shared the same principles.

He said, "I believe an associate of mine is guilty of combustion, in violation of California state law."

"Do you have a name?" I asked.

"Naomi Battle." He said it like it was a name I should know.

"Who is she?"

"Like I said, an associate. A business associate. Some might call her a competitor, but I don't see it that way. We're both striving for the same objective. We'll get there faster if we each know the other is working just as hard to get there first." His gaze strayed to the window behind me. "My father always said it's easy to see others as obstacles, as enemies. It's much harder to admit the only obstacles are your own abilities, the only enemy, your own blindness."

I thought that all sounded very nice. I thought Schuyler could print those words under a photo of a cloud-covered mountain peak and put it in an ornate gilt frame that hung in his entryway so that any dour old ladies who visited would get misty-eyed at the hope that there were still men of substance, of principle, in this decaying world of ours. I said, "Why do you suspect Ms. Battle?"

"I've seen the smoke," Schuyler said. "As the old saying goes, where there's smoke ..."

"You've seen it?"

He pointed through the wall to his right. "Her house is less than two kilometers in that direction. You could see it from here if the mountains weren't in the way."

I went to the window and looked out across the barren, rippling rock to the slope leading to the next denuded peak, then down below to the fire-scalded landscape that provided a buffer between Schuyler and Battle and the artificial light and greenery of the regular rich, and beyond to the Pacific thundering against the sea wall guarding the long-submerged beaches. If anything were burning up here, you'd see it for kilometers around.

I turned to face him and shook my head. "I don't do that. No neighbors, no relatives, no co-workers or business rivals or whatever you want to call them. Nothing personal." I'd made that policy before I took my first private case. Most people are decent enough when left alone. But when you tell some of them that all the rest are criminals and it's up to the rule-followers to enforce the law, that civility quickly goes the way of the manatee. Personal connections only made it worse.

Schuyler leaned back in his chair with his hands behind his head. It wasn't quite the easy, confident motion he probably wanted it to be. It seemed to require some effort for him to shift his bulk into the right position. His mouth went on half-smiling, but his eyes were jade daggers. "Mr. Carver, I'm sure you know the law," he said. "'A person may not knowingly refine, ignite or cause the combustion of hydrocarbon-based or so-called "fossil fuels."' And 'any person, other than an officer or employee of a state or local governmental entity in this state, may bring a civil action against any person who refines, ignites or causes the combustion of hydrocarbon-based fuels in violation of—'"

"I know the law," I said. "It says you may sue Ms. Battle if you believe she's guilty of combustion. It doesn't say I have to help you."

His hands slipped forward from behind his head, and he seemed about to pound his desktop before he got control of himself and laid his palms gently on the smooth gray surface. "It is the moral duty of every upstanding citizen to ensure those who violate the laws of the state are brought to justice."

"That's my policy," I said. "Things get messy when personal feelings are involved." I knew I was crazy to turn my back on a hundred billion dollars. But I was doing it. "Thank you for thinking of me."

Schuyler said nothing, just stared at me with a raised eyebrow and his slowly spreading grin. I waited for a minute, then turned to go.

He let me get to the door. Then he said, "What do you charge for a case like this?"

I stopped. He knew my rate. He must have seen it when he looked me up. But he wanted to hear me say it, wanted me to admit how much I needed the money. I didn't mind. I said, "Two thousand dollars a day, plus expenses."

He tapped his screen and poked at the air above it, manipulating the display he alone could see. "I'm giving you eight thousand for one day. Twenty-four hours, starting right now. If you don't find anything, you keep the money and you never see or hear from me again.

But when you do find something ..." His green eyes glittered as he watched me over fingers steepled against his chin. He angled the point of his hands in my direction. "When you do, you keep working the case for two thousand a day."

I glanced again down the coast. I didn't see any firewalls like the ones that surrounded the wealthy neighborhoods directly below me, and the aquatic filter bots only scrubbed trash and grime out of the water as far as Santa Monica. Beyond that, the sky faded from a clear blue to a murky yellowish gray that mostly obscured the leisure air-liners humming in and out of New LAX. I couldn't see much of the land either—after Beverly Hills, everything blended together in a dirty smear the color of old socks. I pulled up my account and saw the fresh four figures glimmering like dew on a spring morning.

"All right," I said. "Twenty-four hours. I'll let you know if I find anything."

Schuyler raised his chin, and his gaze showed me to the door. "I look forward to hearing from you."

THREE

According to my rental car's nav, it was a six-minute drive to Naomi Battle's house. Plenty of time for my scraper to do its thing. I let the car wind its way down the road from Schuyler's mansion. As soon as the oak trees disappeared from my rear-view mirror, I was transported back into another world. For a brief few moments, here on the edge of one of the biggest cities on the planet, I was alone in the desert. I heard nothing but the murmur of the compressed air engine as my car glided past the barren landscape. Nothing moved. Everything was barren, dusty, dead. The road twisted and rose and fell. On the opposite side of the car, the mountain dropped away, and from my angle, I could see nothing below. The gleaming coast, the lush Palisades, Woods and Hills, even the gray lands beyond, were all gone. I was one wrong turn, one slip of a wheel from plunging into emptiness.

I forced my attention back to the information my scraper had pulled. Naomi Battle: founder and CEO of iRise Space Exploration. Engineering and economics degrees from Stanford. Former Air Force pilot, making her one of the few humans under forty to have actually flown a fighter jet. Left the NASA astronaut training program to start her company, which was recently awarded the contract for the latest Space Exploration for Sustained Human Life mission to Mars. Long-time girlfriend, Chantal Boldin, a fashion designer. Not as rich as Schuyler, but richer than I'd be in a thousand lifetimes.

Gradually, the car snaked its way around one peak and headed up the next until it stopped in front of a rusted metal gate shaped like an elongated right triangle. The barrier looked like an ordinary park road closure, and I had to get out of the car and pretend to be lost while scanning the rocks and chaparral before I spotted a camera embedded in the mountainside abutting the road. I walked to the cliff side of the road and looked up. All I could see was the mountain rising above me. That was as close as I was going to get to Naomi Battle's house without an invitation. I got back in my car and let it take me down out of the park.

On the first residential street below, I parked in front of a weathered, lemon-colored apartment building. Gray balconies wrapped in tinted glass protruded behind the dense foliage of fan palm and fern pine trees. I did some quick research, glancing between the projected display from my screen and a mincing woman leading her tiny prancing dog down the sidewalk. The woman wore a flickering holohead with the supernova-white hair and heavy eye shadow of a füzz singer. The dog looked like a variety of chihuahua, but its holohead had the oversized eyes, floppy ears and short, grinning, tongue-lolling snout of some amalgamated ideal of a puppy. It was about as cute as a pile of intestines tied into a neatly curled bow. What was true in the rest of the country was especially true in La La Land: everybody wanted to be someone else.

I called the listing I had pulled up on my screen.

"iRise Space Exploration," a smooth, synthetic, vaguely feminine voice answered. "How may I help you?"

I chose my words carefully. "Danley Stevens, Pacific Electric. How are you doing today?"

"Very well, thank you for asking. And how are you, sir?"

I dug as deep as an undoped marathoner stumbling across the finish line and summoned as much forced cheer as I could muster. "Great, just great, thank you." I couldn't prove it, but in my experience, a little cordiality worked almost as well to soften up an AI as it did a real live human. The hard approach didn't. Machines don't rattle so easily. "I'm calling about the storm we had last month. The cyclone. Some of our clients experienced issues with their energy supply during that time, either a reduction in power or a complete loss of electricity. Do you recall if you had any problems?"

"No, we didn't," the iRise AI said. "But thank you very much for asking."

"Not a problem," I said. "That's great. I'm glad to hear there was no interruption to your service. Right now, I'm trying to correlate customers who did and didn't experience service interruptions with the age of the customer's electric and climate systems and when those systems were last maintained. Can you tell me when your current systems were installed?"

"One moment, please." The words were only for effect, because my heart hadn't finished its next beat before the AI said, "Our current office space was acquired five years ago. The electrical, heating and cooling systems were retrofitted at that time. Seasonal maintenance on our climate control systems was last performed on March fifth."

"Thank you very much," I said. "That's great. Exactly what I needed to know. Do you happen to know who performed that seasonal maintenance?"

"Let me check." Another brief courtesy pause. "It was CSB Electric and Climate Control."

"Thanks. And just to confirm, your offices are on Lone Oak Road in Los Angeles?" I dangled Battle's home street to see if the machine would bite.

"No sir, we are in downtown Los Angeles. Five fifteen South Figueroa."

"Got it, thank you," I said. "I wonder how that other address got into our system."

The AI didn't take the bait. "Not a problem, sir. Is there anything else I can help you with today?"

"No," I said, "that's all. Thank you for your time."

I called the contact I had for Schuyler. Cherrier gave me the link for Battle's home office. I dredged up my last reserves of courtesy and called it. This time, the male voice that greeted me was human.

"Tayreon Taylor, CSB Electric and Climate Control," I said. "I'm calling to follow up on last month's seasonal maintenance on your cooling system."

"Okay," the man said. "How can I help you?"

"I just wanted to make sure everything is running smoothly. Have you noticed any issues with the climate in the house since that visit?"

"Well, the offices seem to be fine. I don't know about the rest of the house. Hold on. Let me transfer you to someone else."

The next voice introduced herself as Mirlande Joseph. I repeated my introduction.

"Yes, Mr. Taylor," she said in a voice as thin and strong as hydroweb. "Everything seems to be running smoothly. I haven't heard any complaints."

"Excellent," I said. "If you do notice anything, please don't hesitate to reach out."

The holoheaded dog squatted on the sidewalk. The white-haired woman bent down to clean up after it, straining against her too-tight clothing. A torrent of scooter riders surged past us, black mirrored helmets gleaming in the mid-morning sun. Isolated behind her digital mask, the woman watched them as they passed without turning their heads in her direction. The dog wound its way between and around her legs, and she stumbled and caught herself against a tree trunk. I thought there wasn't a better illustration of the world we lived in than this woman wishing people looked at her mediocre holohead while she picked up shit.

I said, "The real reason I'm calling today is to tell you about a new service for premium clients like yourself. It's a complimentary inspection of your entire climate system, top to bottom, inside and out. We want to make sure everything is functioning optimally, that the ducts are clear, the connections are solid, the insulation is airtight. In short, that your home's ecosystem is operating at full capacity day and night, no matter the weather, with no wasted energy that might be costing you extra on your utility bill. As I said, it's completely free of charge. If we see something that could be upgraded, we can discuss suitable options."

I tried to sell my searching pause better than iRise's AI secretary had. "Now, our schedule is filling up, but I have an opening this afternoon if that would work for you. Say two o'clock?"

"Thank you," Mirlande said, "but we don't need—"

"I know, I know," I said. "It sounds like a great way for us to drum up additional business from loyal clients like yourself. That's why the comprehensive inspection is free. No strings attached. If we find anything, we'll send you a full report of the issue. You can take it to any of our competitors and get a quote from them. And if you decide to have us make some adjustments and you don't see the expected savings on your next utility bill, we'll refund you the cost of the service. You have nothing to lose."

"All right," Mirlande said. "But this afternoon won't work."

"No problem," I said. "Let me see here ..." I counted to five. "Oh, look at this. I could fit you in tomorrow morning at ten. How's that?"

"That's fine."

"Great. One of our associates will be at your house at ten sharp tomorrow morning."

By the time I ended the call, my jaw ached from grinning like an idiot for the last fifteen minutes. I massaged my face back into its usual disgruntled state and sent a message to Schuyler letting him know I was putting a hold on our twenty-four-hour arrangement. I'd start the clock again at ten a.m. tomorrow.

FOUR

I spent the night in a Venice Beach motel. The mattress in my room sagged, the sheets were frayed and stained, and the ancient ceiling fan flung a decade's worth of dust off its blades and emitted an odor of burning plastic until it sputtered to a stop around midnight. But I could see a sliver of the ocean between the boxy, featureless backs of the adjacent buildings. I lived a glamorous life.

At five minutes to ten the next morning, I addressed the concealed camera outside the rusted triangular gate blocking the road to Battle's mansion. "Marcus Carver, CSB Electric and Climate Control. I have an appointment."

The gate creaked open. I drove up the mountain road and came to an electrified chain-link fence that matched the disguised state park look of the gate below. A section of the fence swung open for me as I approached. Like Schuyler's place, Battle's mansion was well-hidden by the twisting mountain passes. If you weren't looking for a building, you might not even notice it. It was made of off-white stone and appeared to grow out of the rock. But where the mountain was compact and heavy, the stone of Battle's house seemed delicate and light, rising effortlessly from the peak as though the mountain were a volcano sending up smoke. There were some odes to the old Californian Spanish style architecture in the white stone and understated red clay accents, but the shape was decidedly modern, flowing and vertical instead of sprawling and rectangular.

A tall, slim woman was waiting for me as I stepped out of my car in front of the mansion.

"Good morning, Mr. Carver," she said. She slipped around me and set a black disc on my dashboard. She shut the door, and the car drove off and turned around the side of the house. "I'm Mirlande Joseph, Ms. Battle's chief of staff. Please come in."

Mirlande had large eyes, a long slender neck, and skin as smooth and flawless as molten steel. She wore her hair fashionably short with a bun in the back, and her lips flared outward as if perpetually poised to deliver a gentle kiss. I followed her through the turquoise double front doors and into a white-walled entryway with high ceilings and dark wood support beams. Ahead of me, the room led out to an expansive, verdant courtyard of bladed agave and yucca and the purple, orange and white blooms of desert flowers. The floor was a mosaic of pink and black tiles, and the surrounding cool stone and the gentle breeze coming through the courtyard windows combined to make it feel like I had stepped into a refrigerator.

Mirlande gestured to a squat silver robot waiting inside the door. "Can I offer you anything? Water? Coffee?"

"No, thank you," I said.

She swept one arm toward the elevator. Her movements were graceful, but clipped with precise efficiency. "Where would you like to start?"

"Let's go top to bottom. We'll finish with the courtyard and exterior."

Battle's mansion was roughly U-shaped. The courtyard was in the center, and the open-end of the U faced the ocean to the south. I had entered through the base of the U, on the north side of the house. The mansion had six levels, including a basement. We stepped into a glass elevator that looked out on the mountains to the north. Mirlande pressed the button for the fifth floor, submitted to palm- and retscans, and we took off. The mid-morning sun had surmounted the peaks, and as we ascended, the light caught in the glass and forced me to shield my eyes. On the fifth floor, the elevator door opened behind me.

"This is Ms. Battle's room," Mirlande said.

That was like calling Stonehenge a pile of pebbles. Battle's bedroom was part of a massive suite that occupied the entire top floor. We stepped off the elevator into a sitting area with an L-shaped couch and a holodisplay. Around the corner to the left was the actual bedroom, with a king-sized bed facing a wall of westward windows. Like the rest of the house, the suite followed a sort of elevated Spanish colonial style: clean white walls, touches of exposed wood beams. I had always found buildings of that type to feel rustic and heavy, with the stucco and clay closing in on me and the wood beams the only things keeping me from being buried under a pile of rubble. But in Battle's house, the design felt expansive and airy. I ran my hand over the nearest wall. Upon closer inspection, what looked like stucco-coated adobe was actually some sort of hydroceramic material—just as strong, but a quarter of the thickness of the traditional materials. The walls served their purpose of keeping the house cool during the day and warm at night without conveying the tomb-like feel of brick and plaster. And the cross-laminated timber beams were light and ornamental. In some rooms, including the bedroom, they were carved into arches that seemed to lift the ceiling even farther away from the floor. I assumed the window glass absorbed and released the sun's heat as well, obviating the need for an abundance of insulating walls. The ample sunlight then added to the elegance of the mansion without making it feel stifling. I had met a lot of people who could pay for something that looked good. It took real money to afford something that was even better than it looked.

I had done enough of these civil combustion investigations in the past that I knew what to look for. There probably hadn't been a home with a gas supply built in the last twenty years anywhere in the country. The latest systems were far cheaper and more efficient. If there was anything that would violate the combustion law, it would be something romantic, something nostalgic. A wood-burning fireplace behind a secret panel in the living room, a gas range under a sham stovetop, a grill or fire pit in the courtyard. All of which made the California law sanctimoniously symbolic. The few illicit civilian-owned gas stoves were a drop in the bucket of perfectly legal industrial crude oil. But that law and others like it kept my lights on and put food in my stomach. So there I was.

I started in the bedroom, patting and running my hands along the cool walls to check for hollow spaces. In a suite like this one, I was looking for a concealed fireplace.

"What is this?" I tapped the wall. "Acrylate?"

"I'm not sure," she said. "I know the material is designed to absorb water and expose it to a broad surface area. In hotter temperatures, the water evaporates, cooling the room. In cooler temperatures, the material retains the water to provide insulation."

I nodded. "It's working. Whoever designed this house knew what they were doing."

I continued along the wall to a wide armoire on the far side of the bed. I kneeled down and pretended to examine the wall as I ran my hand along the back of the furniture, searching for a hidden switch or lever.

"Does Ms. Battle spend a lot of time on this floor?" I asked.

"Other than sleeping? I couldn't say." Mirlande leaned over to watch me, her hands clasped behind her back. "I mostly see her during her workday."

"Of course." I stood up and followed the wall to the back of the room. "But it must be nice to come up here and get away from it all at the end of a long day. Kick back, unwind, be alone with your thoughts. I can almost imagine a roaring fireplace back there." I pointed toward the sitting area.

"Yes," she said. "I suppose it is nice."

So far, Mirlande was about as cool as Battle's tall glass windows: transparent enough to let you see the view presented to you, but solid enough to keep out any intrusions.

Beyond the bedroom, the suite divided into a closet and bathroom. The closet was about as big as two rooms in my house, and the bathroom had a full-sized jacuzzi and a steam shower. Mirlande watched from the closet doorway as I pounded the walls more aggressively. They sounded solid. The only thing I was getting was a bruised hand. I made a show of standing in the center of the closet as if feeling the airflow. I crouched and craned to examine the shelves. In the bathroom, I ran the water until it got hot, squatted and felt the pipes under the sink, then ran my hand along the underside of the cabinetry.

"Are you looking for something in particular, Mr. Carver?" Mirlande asked.

I stood and wandered farther into the bathroom. "There are many issues that could affect this home's performance." I rapped on the wall. "Dead spots where the walls aren't absorbing moisture. Poor seals around the windows. Slow-heating water. I'm looking for all of that and more."

When I had finished, Mirlande followed me back through the bedroom and sitting area to the eastern wing, which started with a windowless private art gallery. Battle's tastes were eclectic. There were ancient African masks and modern figures that looked barely human. There were Renaissance oil paintings and chalk cartoons on a blackboard. There were black and white photographs and intricate static holodisplays. Again, I stood in the center of the space, eyes scanning the ceiling, hands spread at my sides. This time, I noticed a slight drop in the temperature.

"Autocustom climate?" I asked.

"Yes," Mirlande said. "Given our location and the house's design, we don't have to run the heating and cooling systems too often. But the entire house is calibrated to Ms. Battle's preferred temperature range. It makes adjustments within that range depending on who else is in a particular room. This gallery is the exception. It always stays on the cooler end of the range to protect the art."

Beyond the art gallery was a second elevator, and beyond that, at the tip of the U's eastern arm and on a level three steps above the rest of this floor, was a set dining table and two chairs. I thought this secluded area would have been an even better spot for a secret fireplace, but there was nowhere to hide one. Floor-to-ceiling windows on all sides showcased a sweeping panorama of the Southern California coast. Unless someone was hauling up logs in the service elevator and building a bonfire on the floor, this level was clean.

I glanced from the window to Mirlande. "Beautiful view."

"Yes, it is." She walked to the end of the room and stood looking back to the northeast. "If you stand here on a clear night, you can see the rockets launching from our space port."

"Ever get drafty in the winter?"

"Drafty?" Her brow pinched into a frown, but there was still a softness in her widened brown eyes and pursed lips. "No, I don't think so. But I'm not up here very often."

We descended to the fourth floor, which contained four guest bedroom suites, each with its own sitting area, workspace, attached bathroom and more modest walk-in closet. If Battle wasn't concealing any combustion violations on her floor, I doubted she had reserved them for her guests. But I checked each room anyway. Only one of them looked occupied—a woman's clothes in the closet and toiletries on the bathroom vanity—but I never saw the occupant.

"How long have you worked for Ms. Battle?" I asked as we waited for the elevator to take us to the third floor.

"Eight years," Mirlande said.

I held the elevator door for her and followed her inside. I noticed she smelled of oranges and bright, clear sunshine. "Do you like it?"

"Yes."

I waited for more, but the elevator doors opened after a brief descent. I exited after her and hesitated in the hallway.

"We're not merely exploring space, venturing into the unknown." Her voice was melodic and polished. I could tell she had spoken those words many times before. "We're building the future. It's exciting to be a part of it." She gestured down the hall, and I fell in step beside her.

The third floor contained a variety of recreation spaces. There was a windowless holodisplay room with tiered reclining lounge seats surrounding the massive display in the center. There was a gym that seemed to have sampled every piece of modern exercise equipment. It had a pair of treadmills and stationary bikes that could tilt upwards, downwards and side to side to simulate hills and banked curves, and each machine was wrapped in a now-transparent holoscreen I assumed would allow the user to feel like they were training anywhere in the world—once they grew tired of the spectacular view through the window in front of them. For days when the sizeable pool I had glimpsed in the courtyard didn't suffice, the gym had a tank large enough for a single swimmer that generated a constant current to keep the user swimming endlessly in place. Like the treadmills and bikes, the sides of the pool were also transparent holoscreens, allowing me to see the display on the bottom that currently projected a vibrant coral reef. Along one wall, there were three benches facing three floor-to-ceiling screens, each set between a pair of cable arms for a variable-resistance strength training machine. And just in case the user wanted to throw around some real objects, there were sets of medicine balls, sandbags and kettlebells of varying weights.

On the other side of the house, there was a game room with a wall of VR headsets, four holoboards and three holodisplays with handheld controllers. Next to it was a meditation room with dim lighting, two float tanks, a stack of yoga mats and even one of those sandboxes monks rake that was decorated with three piles of oval pebbles.

"So what do you really think?" I strolled around the half-lit room, my hands scouring the walls. "About working for iRise and Battle?"

"Like I said—"

"That was the speech you give potential investors." I stepped around a float tank. "It won't help you with me. Everything I have wouldn't get a rocket to San Diego." I looked back at Mirlande and thought I glimpsed the slightest upturn of the left side of her lips.

"I like it," she said. "Really. I met Naomi when she was at NASA. She's—impressive."

Beyond the meditation room was a library with two chaise longues and four recliners, each accompanied by a square side table. In one corner was a fully stocked bar, behind which a four-armed robot waited to take orders. There was even a shelf that took up half of one wall and held what looked like authentic printed books.

I went through my usual charade, checking all the walls before stopping in front of the bookshelf. "Are these real?" I asked.

"Yes," Mirlande said.

"May I?" I gestured at a book. "It's been years since I held one."

"Go ahead."

I pulled out the book and flipped through the pages. There was no hidden compartment. "You said Ms. Battle is impressive." Holding the book open in one hand, I ran my other hand along the underside of the lowest shelf. "Impressive how?" I lifted my head to indicate our surroundings. "Aside from the obvious."

"She's dedicated to this in a way I wasn't." Mirlande watched me with her arms folded over her chest. "In a way few people are dedicated to anything. But I wanted to be a part of it—her company, her mission. And I'm glad I am."

"The world needs people like that." I began tilting books out of the bookcase one at a time. "People who will stop at nothing, who will break the rules to get where they—where we—need to go."

The room was silent for a moment. The atmosphere suddenly felt like a depressurized airtran. I looked back at Mirlande. She had angled her body toward the windows to my left.

"The world needs people like Naomi," she said. She turned toward me and offered a weak smile. "Is there anything else you'd like to see on this level?"

I released the last book and shook my head. "No. Let's continue."

I had taken my time in the meditation room and library, but that floor was clean as well. We descended to the second level, which housed iRise corporate space. There were ten individual offices and a conference room. It was the only above-ground level that had no windows facing the courtyard, but every office had exterior floor-to-ceiling windows looking down on the ocean, the mountains, the forest or the neighborhoods below. We found Battle in her office at the southeast end of the floor, standing behind three one-meter computer displays. She was an imposing woman—broad shoulders, broad hips, muscular thighs that strained the fabric of her slacks. Schuyler's holohead was the face of a regular swimmer, but Battle's figure made her look like she was training for a tryout with the LA-Disney Rams. Like Mirlande, she did not wear a holohead, and she had the wide face and strong pointed chin of an ancient warrior queen.

Mirlande introduced me. Battle nodded a greeting, looked me up and down and returned to her work.

"This will only take a minute, Ms. Battle." I began to circle the room, feeling the walls as I went.

She didn't even glance in my direction. "No problem."

Behind her was a set of shelves dotted with personal memorabilia: degrees earned and honorary, medals, awards, a few photos. I looked at the ceiling as if examining the air and traced one hand along the undersides of the lowest shelves. "Have you noticed any issues with the temperature in the house?"

"No."

From the shelves, I moved to the side wall. "What about last winter? All the heating systems worked to your satisfaction?"

"Yes."

I circled to the front, tapping the walls and glancing back at Battle to study her face through the blue-white light of her computer displays. "Any custom elements in the house?"

Battle flicked her gaze in my direction. "What do you mean?"

I tilted my head at Mirlande. "Ms. Joseph mentioned the autocustom thermostat. I assume that's linked to standard heating and cooling systems. But if there are additional heating elements—or cooling ones—in the house, I'd be happy to check those as well."

Battle's expression remained neutral, but a spark of irritation simmered in her dark eyes. "There is a heat pump for this floor and one for the rest of the house," she said. "Separate accounts. They control the climate in the building."

"Of course," I said. "I'll examine those thoroughly, but if you think—"

"Thank you." Battle forced a close-lipped smile. She had dropped her hands away from her displays and folded them rigidly in front of her. "Ms. Joseph will answer any additional questions you have."

I took my cue to leave. "I'll let you get back to your work. If I find anything, I'll have Ms. Joseph let you know."

Mirlande and I returned to the hallway.

"I see what you mean by dedication," I said.

Mirlande headed back down the hall. "She doesn't like to be interrupted at work." Her voice was brittle and distant as she walked away from me. "I'm sure you can understand."

"Of course." I tapped the courtyard wall with one hand and scanned each office one last time as we passed. "Do you and Ms. Battle always work here?"

"No," Mirlande said. "The main iRise office is downtown. We're there two or three days a week. Or at the spaceport in Mojave if there's a major launch."

Next to the elevator was the utility room devoted to the second-floor corporate space. I was no expert, but I could tell what was what. Heating and cooling, water, electrical—everything checked out.

Mirlande waited by the door while I examined the mechanical elements. "Actually, now that you're here, we have had some problems with the temperature on this floor since last month's service," she said. "Ms. Battle doesn't like to complain, but I've noticed it on warmer days. The service technician did mention there was a part that looked a little worn. The crankcase cooler, I think. Could that be the issue?"

I finished tracing the last line from the heat pump and looked back at her. She had been watching me, but her gaze now cut toward the water heater. I brushed the dust from my hands, and we returned to the hallway.

I checked my screen. "Twenty-two degrees. What do you have?"

Mirlande glanced at her wrist. "Twenty-two."

"Is that within range?" I asked.

"Yes."

"It's still warming up outside," I said, "and the real heat won't hit for another few months. I don't see anything obviously wrong with your system, but if you have issues this summer, let us know and we'll take care of it."

"Okay." Mirlande's eyes were as big as colanders, and she was looking in my general direction without making eye contact. "Thank you."

We boarded the elevator and headed down. Something had changed on the last two floors. I thought about trying to rattle Mirlande a bit more but remembered the role I was playing.

"Do you work every day?" I asked.

"Every day Ms. Battle does."

"From what I can tell, that doesn't give you much down time."

She shrugged as the elevator door opened. I held it for her, and she stepped past me. "You don't strike me as a man who takes many vacations either, Mr. Carver."

"About one a year," I said. "Till I get so bored I can't stand it and I get back to work."

She faced me and gave me a pasted-on smile. "Where would you like to start?"

As Mirlande explained, the ground floor was devoted to entertaining: kitchen, sitting room, ballroom and two dining rooms. I suggested we start with the ballroom, and Mirlande led me there without a word. The massive space occupied the entire west side of the house. There were three balconies on the exterior wall. I walked out onto the first, knowing I probably wouldn't be able to enjoy the view. High, open spaces had never agreed with me. When I reached the balcony railing, I had to squeeze it with both hands at arm's length and lock my legs to keep my knees from buckling. That side of the house overlooked a cliff, and from the balcony, one could look down on a straight drop of at least two hundred meters into the forested area of the park. If there was an exterior fire pit, it wouldn't be on this side of the house.

It took me a few minutes to get a hold of myself on the balcony, and when I returned to the ballroom, Mirlande was studying something on her screen. I hoped that whatever she was looking at was so engrossing that she hadn't witnessed my reaction outside. With Mirlande distracted, I forced myself to peek out at the other two balconies. When I returned a minute later, she was still staring at her screen. I finished inspecting the rest of the ballroom, and Mirlande hurried over to join me at the doorway.

"Ready?" Her voice came out breathy and strained. Her soft features and graceful neck had calcified into a mask of taut skin stretched over the ridges of bone and tendon. She cleared her throat and repeated, "Ready, Mr. Carver?"

I nodded, wondering what she had seen on her screen that had affected her so greatly.

We continued on to the sitting room, the formal dining room that looked like it could seat up to twenty, a more intimate one with a table for six, and the kitchen. While Mirlande's personal chef stood eyeing me with her arms crossed, I spent fifteen minutes inspecting the stove and oven. We did the rest of the ground floor in the same amount of time and descended to the basement.

That level housed quarters for Battle's domestic staff. There were four bedrooms with attached bathrooms, a kitchen and a modest great room with old table tennis and pool tables and a massive holodisplay, along with several well-used but comfortable-looking easy chairs. There was even a set of windows along one wall that offered a view of the Pacific. There was also a massive utility room to supply the residential areas of the house. I saw everything I expected to find, and it all appeared substantial enough for a mansion of this size. I spent ten minutes searching for possible gas lines. But I found nothing amiss. No gas heating. Nothing there that shouldn't have been.

When I had finished, I found Mirlande pacing the great room, her hand trailing across the felt of the pool table, her gaze alternating between the windows and her screen.

"Everything all right?" I asked.

She whirled and stared at me with wide eyes and parted lips. "Huh? Oh, yes. Thank you." She pressed her mouth into a thin smile. "Everything is fine."

I pointed at her screen. "Nothing urgent, I hope."

"What?" She followed my gaze. "Oh, no. Nothing urgent." She forced another smile and extended her arm toward the elevator. "Shall we?"

We returned to the ground floor and exited to the courtyard, a veritable oasis that might almost make a visitor forget they were standing atop a dried-out mountain in the middle of a city fighting off the encroaching desert. Gone was the dry, musty odor of parched earth, replaced by a faint fragrance reminiscent of vanilla and honey. Everything was green and pink and purple, but also tasteful. Only native flora here—no water-guzzling irises or hibiscuses or dense shade trees. The structure of Battle's house warded off the harshest sunlight, and there were ample umbrellas and canopies for when the summer sun was at its apex. The swimming pool was in the center—close to twenty meters long and dwarfed by the surrounding mansion. Next to it was a jacuzzi big enough that you'd have to use signal flags to communicate with the person seated across from you. Around the pool were a dozen lounge chairs, and at the southern end of the courtyard was a dining table with six seats. But once again, nothing illicit. No fire pit, no firewood, no grill, no trapdoors, hidden switches or secret wall panels.

When I reached the end of the courtyard, I looked back to see Mirlande waiting at the door to the house. She stood as stiff as a convict at a conjugal visit, her hands clenched behind her back. As I approached, she turned on her heel and led me inside. We passed through the house and exited to the front. Compared to the courtyard, the exterior landscaping was minimal, lending to the impression that the mansion was a natural extension of the mountain. As I had observed from the ballroom, the mountain dropped away from the western side of the house with no space between the exterior wall and the cliff. Mirlande waited for me at the front and led me briskly around the eastern side of the house to a massive two-story garage. My car sat out front, along with six others I suspected belonged to Battle's domestic staff or iRise employees. Inside the garage were eight vehicles, all in black: a sporty convertible, a muscular sedan and two sturdy SUVs on the ground level, and four flyers on the upper level beneath overhead sectional doors. I inspected each vehicle. I recognized each of the models, and none of them ran on gasoline. I searched the rest of the building, looking for hidden doors or panels concealing a classic gas automobile—an impractical sentimentality that would mean somehow procuring cans of fuel to keep on hand—but found nothing. Back outside, I walked the perimeter of Battle's mansion, noting the pair of outdoor units for her two heat pumps. More importantly, I saw no gas meter or lines.

All told, it took us almost two hours to cover every room in Battle's mansion. But I found nothing. No fireplace, no gas stove, no fire pit, no grill. No false ranges or secret wall panels. No chimneys on the exterior, no gas ducts in the utility rooms. Battle's home surely consumed a tremendous amount of energy, but as far as I could tell, she was connected to the regular grid, and that meant it was all clean. If Schuyler had seen any smoke, it was from hitting his hubble a little too hard. I thanked Mirlande for her time, told her everything looked in order and asked her to call if the second-floor temperature went rogue again. She nodded woodenly and walked me back to my car.

FIVE

Mirlande removed the black disc from my car's dashboard, and I got in and drove off. I estimated it was nearly a kilometer from Battle's mansion to the rusted triangular gate. When I was about halfway between the chain-link fence and the gate and could no longer see the house in my rearview mirror, I let the car go around the next bend in the mountain and then pulled over behind a boulder. I got out, leaned against the trunk of the car and waited. I didn't know what I was waiting for. But something told me to wait, and I did.

The winds were whipping across the mountains and down toward the coast, driving away any trace of clouds and leaving me to broil under the midday sun. It must have been nearly ten degrees warmer than when I'd arrived at Battle's that morning, and I had dressed for a balmy spring day instead of an oven. To the north, I could see the billowing smoke of the distant wildfires, and there was an acrid odor in the air, a mixture of ash and melted plastic. Around me, the mountains spread out like a giant, twisted, three-fingered hand clawing southward into the earth. Schuyler's mansion was on the eastern knuckle, Battle's on the western one, with an unadorned finger in between. I was standing on the slope of Battle's ridge, low enough that I couldn't see Battle's mansion above, nor Schuyler's ridge behind the rise of the middle claw.

After about ten minutes, two events happened to reward my patience. First, I heard the patter of dust against the roof of my car.

About five meters above me, a man was creeping along one of the park's old hiking trails. He was dressed in a lightweight desert camouflage jacket and matching pants. His hair was long and unkempt, and the fact that he appeared to take his infrequent showers in a sandstorm helped his efforts to blend in. As I watched him, he crouched and signaled with his arm toward the middle ridge. A figure in a matching dust-caked costume moved along the opposite slope. I ducked behind the car. Whether or not the second figure saw me, they didn't seem to care. After a moment, the man above me continued in the direction of Battle's house, and the figure across the valley moved in parallel. When the man had put some distance between us, I headed back up the road toward the house, keeping myself as close to the mountain as possible. I got no more than twenty steps before I heard a distant hum overhead and saw a flyer taking off from where I knew Battle's house was. I returned to my car immediately and directed it down the mountain road.

I had rented the low-slung Kwang Automotives sedan at the airtran depot. The automated teller had bragged about the range of the vehicle's compressed air engine. I asked if it would go on green and stop on red. The gentle synthetic voice assured me it did. There's no use getting cute with service AI. I reached the gate, which opened automatically as I approached, and drove down out of the mountains to the main road below. There, I spotted the flyer from Battle's house overhead, bearing southeast. I aimed my screen at it and captured a hi-res image of its registration number. It was useless trying to follow it on surface roads, so I entered a location fifteen kilometers southeast into the Kwang's onboard nav system. The car accelerated, following the expected course of the vehicle above me. With the Kwang's speed limit control, I had no chance of catching the flyer, but I hoped to hang close enough to see where it landed.

The Kwang turned left and drove along the coast, sandwiched between the dusty cliffs and the turquoise waves lapping at the rocks below. It hummed along smoothly, changing lanes and anticipating traffic signals to avoid unnecessary slowdowns. The road plunged to sea level, and an arcing glass wall rose on my right and stretched overhead to protect the street from the encroaching ocean. Skyduster palm trees and gleaming houses whiter than wedding dresses dotted the bluffs above, and the surf pressed itself against the glass gently, insistently. A few solitary seagulls wheeled in the wake of Battle's flyer, scanning for crumbs on the porches and restaurant patios overlooking the ocean. Up ahead, the mountains yielded to a freeway that slashed inland. To the right of the road, a dilapidated paddleboat sat moored against the shore, bearing the name "Santa Monica Pier," though most of the restaurants and attractions that lined its decks appeared closed for good. Beyond it, the half-submerged spokes of the monument marking the old pier's Ferris wheel stabbed out of the empty cobalt expanse.

The Kwang swung left onto the freeway and headed east. The cars were packed tighter than an East Asian fish farm, but with every car linked to the freeway network, traffic flowed as easily as the ocean behind us. Almost immediately, the high-rises that lined the shore disappeared, giving way to long, low warehouses and the stumps that marked the entrances to subter residences. People like Schuyler and Battle could pay for seclusion. Even the regular rich could hide behind their holoheads in their gated communities in the foothills, and the possibility of an ocean view was still enough to make others forgo that security. The middle class didn't have that luxury. For them, privacy meant living where even the sun and fresh air couldn't find them. But the shift in demographics gave me a clear view overhead, and from the five flyers headed in my direction, I quickly identified Battle's ahead of me on the left.

Unfortunately for me, it appeared to be traveling almost twice as fast as I was. If it veered away from the freeway or was traveling more than thirty kilometers, I would lose it. Around me, the landscape faded from green and blue and white to brown and gray. At the same time, the surroundings grew brighter, the sunlight stronger. Just as the Kwang's interior became stifling under the midday sun, the climate control system adjusted with a welcome blast of cool air. Gaudy holodisplays arched overhead, their advertisements changing with each wave of passing cars. In my rental, I saw overstimulating theme parks, nightlife glittering too brightly, and hikers and beachgoers grinning vapidly. The downtown skyline rose on my left, a forest of overlapping, cold, featureless, mirrored glass spires. Jumpers flitted past the distant buildings, carrying passengers across town. The freeway crossed the trickle of the Los Angeles River, and the garish lights of a casino assaulted my eye, somehow outshining the sunlight that had bleached everything else. Up ahead, the flyer banked to the right. The Kwang continued for another kilometer, then exited in East LA and headed south.

The street ran between densely packed, fiber-sidinged houses with darkened windows surrounded by walls covered by dead ivy and a dusty cemetery with gravestones rising like the rib bones of beasts that had succumbed to the desert. Anonymous, tinted-windowed cars zipped past, but the street was devoid of pedestrians. The Kwang turned left and entered a commercial district of single-story brown storefronts with striped awnings stretching out over empty sidewalks lined with leafless trees.

Ahead, Battle's flyer circled and descended, giving me time to close the gap. I was two blocks away when it landed, and the Kwang neared it in time for me to see a figure emerge, wearing a holohead and dressed in a long, beige, shapeless trench coat. If I hadn't spent the last two hours following Mirlande around Battle's mansion, I never would have recognized her. I took control of the wheel and eased as close as I dared. But Mirlande didn't bother looking around her. She headed straight for a storefront across the street and went inside.

I sat in the car and scanned the street. It wasn't two minutes before another car approached from the opposite direction and parked in front of the storefront where Mirlande had entered. A man in a holohead that reminded me of screen star Jhonny Rodriguez got out and went into the shop. I put on the holohead I kept in my pocket. Even with the omnipresent cameras in every corner of the country, I preferred not to wear it. I never got used to people I knew looking at me like I was a stranger. But of course, that was the whole point of the thing. And I didn't want Mirlande to recognize me now. I got out of my car, walked to the shop and stood there pretending to look at my screen while glancing through the window. It was an electronics store—used devices and repairs—and looked like a front.

Inside, Mirlande stood at a display next to the man from the second car. It was an older store—no alkaloided sales models showing off the latest screens or pushy interactive holodisplays tailored to each customer, just a few rows of shelves with mostly outdated gadgets. Mirlande and the man faced the shelves and appeared to be examining the merchandise, but I could see their lips moving in conversation. I turned to bring my screen as close to the store window as possible and switched on the recording mike as high as it would go. But it wasn't enough. The window must have been made from some kind of reinforced polymer. After a moment, the two concluded their conversation, and Mirlande drifted away.

I returned to my car. Mirlande exited the shop. She was more cautious this time, pausing outside the door to look up and down the street before walking briskly back to her flyer. A minute later, the man exited and returned to his car. I let him get a block away before I pulled out and followed him.

SIX

I gave the Kwang a break and took over the wheel. It was a short-lived break. Mirlande's contact made a quick right. I hung back a bit and picked him up again after I turned the corner. We drove down a barren boulevard of empty lots and wary one-story houses with patchy lawns surrounded by chain-link fences. After half a kilometer, he pulled into the left turn lane. I let another car get between us and swung out wide on the turn to keep him in view. We passed squat stone buildings baking under the broad gray sky and brightly colored businesses with chipped and peeling paint. I kept my distance, occasionally ducking behind dingy blue and orange buses carrying dead-eyed faces leaning against the windows. After another half-kilometer, he pulled over and parked. I made a quick right and stopped, watching him in my side mirror. He got out, crossed the street to a long brick building and went inside.

I stepped out of the car and walked as casually as I could to the opposite corner and down the street to the building. There were three addresses, each with blinds drawn over the glass of the window and doors. When I had almost passed the first address where Mirlande's contact had entered, I made a sharp left to the door and knocked. There was no answer. I waited for a minute, then knocked again, louder and longer. After another minute, the lock clicked, and the door cracked open. I saw the sliver of an expressionless holohead—not the one I had been following.

When he didn't speak, I said, "I'm looking for somebody." I held up a hand at the height of my forehead. "This tall, skinny, sometimes wears a holo that looks like Jhonny Rodriguez. See if he remembers shooting craps at Caesars with me last night. Ask if he left something behind." I winked. "His good luck charm."

"Wrong address." The door closed swiftly, but I was quick enough to get both hands up and stop it.

"You sure?" I gritted my teeth and put on the smile of a man who had never lived in the real world. "Maybe I'm forgetting the holo. It was a big night. Ask your friends in there if any of them remember Jaden Johnson."

This time, I wasn't fast or strong enough to keep the door open. The lock clicked again to confirm my visit was over.

I stepped back to the edge of the sidewalk to have a look at the place. The building was at least a hundred years old. Red brick with a concrete overhang to ward off the sunlight against the glass windows and doors. On closer examination, what looked like vinyl blinds were actually white-painted metal security shutters. The same shutters obscured the windows of the other two addresses in the building. It was a location designed to avoid attention and to discourage anyone who got close enough from feeling too curious. I had a fair idea of what was happening behind those doors—and on the floors below—and they weren't selling insurance.

I went back to my car and found a place for a late lunch. I paid eighty dollars for a pair of turkey sandwiches and one-fifty for a bottle of Japanese whisky at the liquor store next door. I ate the first sandwich while the Kwang drove me back to the electronics shop. It wasn't bad. I knew it was all lab grown, but it tasted like the real thing. But those ag scientists were still missing something. Maybe being alive and outside under the sun at one point instead of in Petri dishes and tanks made all the difference.

The electronics store was the same kind of unassuming place as Mirlande's friend's building. There were no shimmering holodisplays on the roof or the sidewalk out front. No one inside was loudly demonstrating the latest upgrade to a cluster of twittering shills. In fact, I didn't see any merchandise that looked less than five years old. Most people probably passed the place without giving it a second glance. But for anyone wise to the spot, the overabundant shelves of obsolete crap offered space for quiet conversations, and I could tell from the fraction of the building's footprint devoted to retail that there was plenty of room in the back to conduct the place's real business. When I entered, the only other person inside was a woman behind the counter who eyed me in silence from the moment I cracked open the door until I stopped in front of her. She wore no holohead, which I figured was an effort to make it look like she had nothing to hide.

"Help you?" she asked.

"Yeah." I rested my hands on the counter and scanned the products on the wall behind her. "You got a used nav? Nothing fancy. Just something to get me to an appointment so I don't have to wait for repair uploads."

She peeled herself off her seat and trudged to a shelf near the front of the store.

"Here." She handed me a nav that was at least two decades old, one of those models that had a brief spike when a handful of people refused to get screens or smart cars. She sniffed and rubbed her nose. "One-ten."

"Mind if I try it?" I asked.

She gave me a look that said she was using every gram of strength to hold back an eye roll and exasperated sigh. "Address?"

I gave her the address of where I had lost Mirlande's friend. That got a reaction. Her fingers froze above the nav screen. Her eyes searched my face.

"You know it?" I asked.

She shook her head, looked down and punched in the address. The route and directions matched the trip I had just made. "It's one-ten," she said. "You want it?"

"Sure." I pretended to admire the rest of her merchandise. "Listen, I'm not from around here. I came into town for a deal. That's the address. I'd like to know what I'm walking into."

She crossed her arms and watched me like I was an interminable update wheel. "One-ten."

"All right." I tapped my screen. "I'm sending two hundred on account of the excellent service. For telling me about that address."

She stared back at me. "The nav costs one-ten." After that slip when I gave her the address, she had put her bored salesclerk mask back on and kept it in place. Either she was too thick to get what I was offering, or it was going to take a lot more than ninety dollars to squeeze it out of her. I didn't think it was the former.

"All right," I said. "Guess I'll find a nav somewhere else."

I returned to my car and headed back toward the coast. At the very least, my limited conversation with the electronics girl had confirmed two things. One, Mirlande was dealing with people decent folks don't mix with. Two, whatever she was up to, it had nothing to do with my case. The black market for hydrocarbon fuels was so small that no one cared to corner it. If you wanted a gas line for your fancy antique stove, you didn't need a secret meeting with a man who worked in a place everyone was too afraid to talk about.

Back when I was still a police detective, I got assigned to Homicide shortly after the murder of Dareon Pfenning. Pfenning had been a prominent community leader and anti-violence activist, an outspoken critic of the Stone Kings and other Chicago gangs. When he called for a boycott of a list of businesses suspected to be Stone fronts, the Stones had him killed. A week after his murderer was convicted, Lucia Williams, the little old lady who gave eyewitness testimony at the trial, wound up dead as well. Her body was found in the middle of Ashland Avenue with her screen display projecting "SNITCH" above her corpse. No witnesses came forward to identify her killer. Her case was never solved. That gave me an idea of the kind of people

I was dealing with in LA. Because a place like that electronics store would have been at the top of Pfenning's list.

The Kwang followed the crowded freeway back through the city. Maybe it was my westward vantage point, but the plumes of black smoke in the mountains to the northwest seemed thicker and darker than they had four hours ago. The sun was a broken egg yolk oozing into the Pacific by the time I hit the Santa Monica foothills, and it disappeared behind the mountains as I wound my way upward toward Battle's house. I pulled under a stand of oak trees and turned off the car. From that spot, I could see the crest of the ridge where Battle's house was, the rusted gate on the edge of her property and the face of the adjacent ridge where I had spied the camouflaged figure earlier that day. I still didn't know what I was looking for. Probably nothing. Whatever was going on at that house, I doubted it had anything to do with me. But Schuyler had hired me for twenty-four hours. So I opened the whisky, ate my other sandwich and settled in for the night.

SEVEN

The gunfire had stopped, and an eerie quiet had settled over the Chicago streets. A crimson sun poked its head above the low, worn stone buildings and mangled, sagging trees, while a cold slate sky pushed back against the dawn, warning the sun to stay down. I was standing at the corner of 47th and Morgan, staring at the pair of corpses at my feet. The two bodies wore identical black uniforms, sky blue helmets and matching holoheads. The blood from their head wounds had escaped their digital masks to form ruby necklaces around their throats. But somehow I knew the one on the right was the real Julia Noi, the one on the left an imposter. I felt myself moving toward Julia, the latest in an endless tide of bodies that stretched back to Williams, Pfenning and beyond. I knew what I would see under that mask, but I couldn't stop myself. I kneeled in the silent, empty street and reached for the holo unit on her collarbone.

I awoke to a film of ash coating the hood of my car. The sun had just crested the mountain ridge to the east, curling fingers of light up over the peak and down into the valley between us, when an unmarked police car breezed past me and headed up the road toward Battle's mansion. I started the Kwang and followed it, allowing the curving mountain road to shield me from the other vehicle and accelerating past the triangular gate and through the gap in the chain-link fence before they closed behind me. I stopped on the side of the road out of view of Battle's house and waited five minutes to allow whatever was going to happen to start happening.

When I approached the house on foot, there was no one around, and the cop's car was parked in front of the garage. I entered the house through the front door.

"I know we covered this before," the cop was saying, "but have you heard anything from Mr. King? Any idea of where he might have gone that night? Anything he planned to do? Anyone he planned to meet?"

I closed the door softly behind me.

Over the cop's shoulder, Mirlande's glimmering eyes darted to me while Battle fixed me with an icy glare.

The cop, a plainclothes detective, turned to face me. "Can I help you?" He was a slump-shouldered, heavyset man who had somehow never acquired a Southern California tan.

"Excuse me, Ms. Battle, Ms. Joseph," I said. "Something occurred to me last night. The airflow in your third-floor library—I'd be letting you down if I didn't check it out. I know I should have called, but I was in the area ..."

The cop glanced from me to Battle.

Battle sighed and whispered something to Mirlande, who led me to the elevator while avoiding eye contact.

"Busy morning," I said as we ascended to the third floor.

"Yes," Mirlande said to the elevator doors. "Tragic." Her voice had that distant quality you hear on old audio recordings, where it sounded like the speaker was at the bottom of a lake.

We exited the elevator, and I followed Mirlande down the western corridor. "Did the police say what happened to this Mr. King?"

"They found his body below the Seventh Street Bridge."

I had spent most of the night considering the possible ramifications of everything I learned the previous day. But I hadn't expected a dead body to accompany the dawn. "Was it suicide?" I asked.

"They don't know."

I shook my head sympathetically and offered my condolences. In the library, I made a show of feeling the air and checking my screen repeatedly. Then I walked to the west window and ran a hand along the seal. I imagined the cop downstairs, assembling Battle's staff, asking if they knew anything about King's last whereabouts. I wanted to kill just enough time to be there when the party broke up. "How well did you know him?" I said.

"Well enough."

Her voice behind me was hardly more than a whisper. I glanced over my shoulder. She was turned away from me, and her gentle shoulders were hunched, her thin arms hugging her chest as though if she squeezed hard enough, she might actually make herself disappear.

She met my gaze briefly, then turned away again. "He was Ms. Battle's head of security."

Her face in that instant was stripped bare, her wide, dark eyes, high, hard cheekbones and full, scarcely parted lips forming a naked font of emotion that appeared capable of any reaction. It felt almost indecent to look at her.

"Had he been missing for a while?" I said to the window.

"Yes," she said. "Almost two weeks."

Below me, the ballroom balconies jutted out over the cliff. Even behind a sheet of glass, it was a dizzying sight, those little life rafts dangling above the maw of the shadowed gorge. For some reason, it made me think of Mirlande in her holohead and trench coat walking into that electronics shop.

"It sounds like he got in over his head," I said. "He thought he knew what he was doing, but he trusted the wrong people. People who can't be trusted with anything." I glanced over my shoulder. Mirlande had not moved. "By the time he realized it was too late, there was nothing he could do to get himself out."

The silence behind me was as fathomless as the darkened chasm below. In the distance, the morning sun cast the rolling mountain ridges in bands of light and shadow. I started to walk the perimeter of the room.

"You don't work for CSB," Mirlande said. "Do you?"

I kept moving, tracing a hand along the wall, and glanced at Mirlande from the corner of my eye. "Do you need to see my ID?"

Her arms still hugged her chest, and she was gazing toward my back with unfocused eyes. "There's no such thing as a crankcase cooler," she said. "Not in heat pumps, anyway."

I continued past the bookshelf, weighing my next move. Then I stopped and faced her. "You're right. I'm a private detective."

The revelation made as much of an impression on her as a speck of dust falling against the mountain we stood on. Whatever was going through her mind had hardened her against any new blows. Finally, she said, "Are you finished here?"

I held her gaze. She dropped her hands to her sides, raised her chin and stared back at me with feverish, over-bright eyes. "Sure," I said. "For now."

We descended to the ground floor in silence. By the time we arrived in the entry foyer, the assembled staff members were indeed dispersing.

The cop looked in our direction. "Ms. Joseph," he said, "I'd like a minute of your time, please."

Mirlande walked briskly toward him.

"You done here?" he called to me.

"Sure," I said. "You want to get some coffee? My treat."

He fixed me with an unblinking gaze I figured was supposed to make career criminals break down and confess to torturing the neighbor's cat when they were nine years old. I looked back at him in silence.

He cocked his head toward the front door. "Get out of here."

I turned and went. When I stepped outside, I saw a woman standing by the stone barrier at the cliff edge of the driveway. I recognized her from the previous day's investigation as Battle's personal chef. She glanced at me when I came up beside her but said nothing and went back to staring into the abyss.

I followed her gaze, decided I didn't like where it was headed and shuffled back a step. "You holding up okay?" I asked.

"Fine." She sipped from a tumbler containing what I guessed was tequila.

"Were you close?" I asked. "With Mr. King?"

She laughed, a short, derisive, barking noise. "He was an asshole."

"How so?"

She studied my face over the rim of her glass. "You were here yesterday. Poking around my kitchen."

"That's right."

"I thought you were an electrician or something."

"Or something."

Her eyes narrowed. "You here about King?"

"Should I be?"

She shrugged. "The police were here two weeks ago, after he disappeared. They're back today to say he's dead. Now that they have a body, I guess they'll figure out what happened."

I gazed across the undulating western landscape, where a string of pearly white houses curved along the coast and into the valley before another distant ridge. To the north, I could see the billowing black smoke from the distant fire, and I could smell the charred odor on the wind. "You said he was an asshole."

She turned back to the cliff and sipped her drink. "He liked women," she said, "and 'no' didn't seem to mean much to him."

"He ever get rough with you?" I asked.

She shook her head.

"What about with anyone else in the house?"

"I don't know. He'd make comments. Try to grab a girl's ass when he thought no one else could see."

"Anyone ever say anything to Ms. Battle?"

"Two years ago." She cradled the glass in both hands and gazed out over the sun-dappled ridges. "King was after Naomi's trainer at the time. Her name was Jordan. Jordan Thompson. We told her to go to Naomi. I don't know if she ever did, but one day she was gone and Connell fucking King was still here. I suppose he's good at his job. Was good at his job. And a very convincing liar."

"You tell all that to the detective?" I asked.

She met my gaze. "He didn't ask."

"What did he ask?"

"If I'd heard anything from King since his disappearance. If I knew where he was going. Or who he might have been meeting." She swirled her drink and stared at the ice as it clinked against the glass. "I don't know any of that."

"Thank you, Ms. ..."

"Giménez," she said. "Camila."

"Thank you, Camila."

I left her to her drink and walked back down the dusty road to my car.

EIGHT

That should have been the end of it. It had been forty-eight hours since I accepted Schuyler's offer. I should have followed the winding mountain roads back to his mansion and told him he was mining the wrong salt bed. But I didn't. Instead, I waited until the detective's car passed me on its way down, and I drove back up to Battle's house.

The front door was still unlocked. Things had really gotten lax since Battle's head of security ran off and died. Mirlande and Battle stood in the entry hall, speaking in hushed voices. Mirlande saw me first. She hurried over to head me off, but I spoke up before she could make it halfway.

"Excuse me, Ms. Battle. I think it's time to come clean. My name is Marcus Carver. But I don't work for an electric and climate company. I'm a private detective." I showed her my license. "I've been working with Ms. Joseph."

It was a gamble, but I figured there had to be a reason Mirlande hadn't given me up yet. It paid off. Mirlande's eyes blazed at me with a fire I hadn't seen in them before, but she stopped, composed herself and turned back to Battle.

"He's been investigating Connell's disappearance," she said. "When the police didn't come up with anything, I thought we could use some outside help, and I wanted to keep you out of it in case there were any unseemly discoveries."

Battle eyed us, her jaw clenched.

"Unfortunately," I said, "we no longer have that luxury. I have some theories about what happened to Mr. King, but at this point, I need to ask you some questions."

Battle's gaze settled on me and stayed there. "You were in my office yesterday."

"I needed to get a sense of how you would handle things."

"And?"

"And I was right. You need to know what's happening so you can deal with it your way."

Battle studied me with her arms crossed. She blew out a long exhale. "All right," she said. "Come upstairs."

We rode the elevator to the second floor in silence. Battle stood with her back to me, feet spread, hands on her hips, looking out at the mountains to the north. When the elevator stopped, she spun past me and strode down the hall to her office. She sat behind her desk and indicated a vacant chair on the opposite side.

"Ms. Joseph told me most of what happened." I lowered myself into the chair. "But I'd like you to confirm some details."

Battle raised her eyebrows. "Such as?"

"Mr. King went missing two weeks ago, correct?"

"Almost two weeks." Battle leaned back in her chair. Her hands gripped the armrests, and she measured each word with an engineer's precision. "April fourth. So twelve days ago."

"How did you become aware of his disappearance?" I asked.

"I didn't see him at the end of his shift that night." Her right index finger picked at her armrest. "But I didn't think anything of it until he didn't show up the next day."

"On April fifth."

"Yes."

"How does Mr. King get to and from your house?"

"He drives himself."

"In his personal car?"

"Yes."

"Was his car here—"

Battle leaned forward and folded her hands atop her desk. "Mr. Carver, surely Ms. Joseph told you all of this already. Why do you—"

"Everyone tells it a little differently," I said. "Each person offers details another doesn't remember or doesn't think worth mentioning." I could tell Battle wasn't used to being interrupted. But I didn't give her time to complain about it. "Was Mr. King's car here the day he didn't show up for work?"

Battle held my gaze, her folded hands still clenched. "Yes."

Battle may have been tough, but I was starting to like her. She had work to do and she needed everyone around her to do their own jobs or stay out of her damn way so she could get on with it. "Do you know if it ever left between April fourth and fifth?" I asked.

She continued staring through me and shook her head. "From what my new head of security tells me, no. Mr. King's car has been here since the fourth."

"When did the police get involved?"

"Ms. Joseph notified the police the day after we noted Mr. King's absence. April sixth."

"So between April sixth and today, did you have any contact with the police? Did they provide any updates?"

"They sent a copy of the missing person report." Battle unfolded her hands and brushed an invisible speck of dust off her desk. "Other than that, no."

"When was the last time you saw Mr. King in person?" I asked.

"The night of April fourth," she said. "We had a party to celebrate the Seashell contract."

I cocked an eyebrow. "Seashell?"

"SESHL. Space Exploration for Sustained Human Life." She offered a slight grimace. "It's contrived, I know. Anyway, I spoke to Mr. King early on that night. Maybe around five-thirty or six. Just long enough for him to let me know everything was in order. I might have seen him at other times throughout the night—I'm not positive. But that was the last time I spoke to him."

"How many people were at the party?" I asked.

"About two hundred fifty."

"Do you have a guest list?"

"I'll make sure you get one." Battle's stare was no less direct, but its edge had softened slightly.

"I assume there are security cameras around this house," I said.

"There are."

"Are your employees tracked?"

"No." Battle sat back in her chair and drummed one set of fingers against the armrest. "Access to certain parts of the house is limited depending on the person's role. Some only have access to the second floor. Some, like Ms. Joseph and Mr. King, have access to the entire house. All my employees are vetted before they're hired. But once they're here, I don't track any of them."

"Did any of the cameras capture Mr. King exiting the house?"

"No. Not that I'm aware of."

I settled back in my chair and said, "As I was leaving yesterday, I saw one of your flyers take off. Was that you?"

"No." Battle sighed. "I was here all day."

"One of your employees then?"

"It must have been." Her hands returned to their tight fold.

I sensed my time was limited. I could appreciate that. But I wasn't done yet. "Does that happen often?" I asked. "One of your employees taking a vehicle without notifying you?"

She shrugged. "It happens. I trust my staff to do what they need to further the company's goals. Sometimes they have appointments or unforeseen circumstances that require their attention in the middle of the day. Flyers are usually the most efficient means of travel. Especially from this location."

"Of course," I said. "It was probably unrelated. In my experience, it's worth asking about everything, no matter how insignificant it appears." I rested my hands on the arms of my chair. "All right. Let me make sure I have this straight. Sometime between the night of April fourth and the morning of April fifth, Connell King disappeared. If he was still in this house on April fifth or later, no one saw him. If he left the house, he didn't do it in his own car. And no one has admitted to seeing him leave, knowing where he went or with whom. Is that right?"

"That's right."

I stood. "I'd like to see the security footage from the night of April fourth."

"Fine." Battle rose and led me down the hall to the first office on the west side of the floor. "This is Dev Chaudhri." She indicated the skeletal man hunched over his desk. "Mr. King's replacement."

Chaudhri stood up too quickly, banging his thighs against the underside of the desk.

"Dev," Battle said, "Mr. Carver here would like to see the security footage from the night of April fourth. Give him anything he needs."

She exited to the hallway, and I walked around the desk to stand behind Chaudhri.

"I've tracked Mr. King throughout the night until here." Chaudhri spoke fast enough to outpace one of Battle's rockets, and his right leg bounced rapidly under his desk as he worked. He pointed to the still image of a bald, square-jawed man on his computer display. "After that, he gets lost among the other guests." Chaudhri let the footage play, and King immediately slipped behind a woman with an updo that could have housed every bee left in the world.

"This is in the ballroom, right?" I asked.

"Yes."

I tried to follow the line King had taken, but he never reappeared. The big-haired woman moved in the direction he had been heading, but when she stopped to chat with a short, squat man with his back to the camera, King was nowhere to be seen.

I glanced at the clock on the display: 20:32. "Go back," I said. "Let me see where he's coming from."

We followed King in reverse until the camera lost him. Chaudhri pulled up another angle that tracked King back to the ballroom entrance and let the video play. King prowled in, head pivoting to scan the guests in the room. He edged through the crowd without speaking to anyone. Eventually, he made his way to a bar on one side of the ballroom. The robot bartender poured him a drink—liquor, neat—and he drank it down in two gulps. He ordered a second and took it with him as he re-entered the throng of guests.

"He's moving west, right?" I asked.

"Yes," Chaudhri said.

We lost him again at 20:32.

"Got another angle?" I asked. "A camera on the west wall?"

Chaudhri shook his head. "I checked all the angles. All the cameras in the house. This is the last time he appears on video."

"And the exterior cameras?"

"Nothing. I ran a facial recognition search. The last image the system recognizes is right here. Plus, I spent the past week watching exterior footage from eight-thirty to midnight. I didn't spot him either."

"Go back again to where we lose him," I said, "and let it play."

King disappeared about ten meters from the doors to the northwest balcony. The big-haired woman finished her conversation and moved on. The short man headed east. Two other men, one with a woman on his arm, approached the balcony. Most of the guests turned toward the southern end of the room.

"The band starts playing again now," Chaudhri said.

The two men and the woman walked out to the balcony. A pair of women followed a few seconds later.

I pointed at the exit to the balcony. "Got a camera out there?"

"We did," Chaudhri said. "It was damaged during the cyclone last month. It hasn't been fixed yet. But have you seen the balconies?"

I knew what he meant. There wasn't much to secure on that side of the house. Anyone wanting to break in from the cliff side would have an easier time cracking the federal digital reserve.

"What about the other balconies?" I asked. "Those cameras still work?"

"Sure. Here's one." Chaudhri paused the video and pointed to a second display showing an overhead view of six guests standing on another balcony. The fixed camera captured the length and width of the balcony and not much else.

"All right." I pointed to the display we had been watching. "Keep playing this one."

About a third of the guests drifted toward the dance floor at the southern end of the room. The rest took advantage of the extra space. Conversation groups shifted away from one another. Several people headed toward the bar. A man and woman approached the northwest balcony, glanced outside and liked the view as much as I did. The female couple followed them back inside.

The short man was speaking animatedly to a wispy woman half his age. She bobbed her head politely and looked around for someone to save her. Almost everyone turned toward the band as they apparently struck up a popular tune. The male and female couple returned from the balcony and headed for the dance floor. The balcony doors closed behind them. An eager young man in a suit too large for him rescued the bored young woman and led her off to dance. Several more guests followed them.

"Did you know him?" I asked.

"King?" Chaudhri said. "Sure. He hired me."

"What did you think of him?"

Chaudhri looked up at me. His leg stopped bouncing. "He was good at what he did. But he mostly worked days, and I worked nights. Our paths didn't cross much."

"Any idea where he might have gone?"

He shrugged. "If I knew anything, we wouldn't be doing this."

On Chaudhri's display, a man looked through the closed balcony doors, then opened one and stepped outside. Two women followed him. A woman in a gray dress returned from the balcony. I recognized Mirlande immediately. She stopped inside the doors and looked around the room. Then she walked, tentatively at first, then faster and faster, across the room, slipping between the other guests until she was swallowed up by the crowd.

Two older couples exited to the balcony. The single man came back in. The short man stood alone, hands in his pockets, looking around for someone else to bore. When he didn't find any suitable targets, he gave up and headed for the bar. People drifted back from the dance floor, the hit song having evidently come to an end.

Chaudhri glanced at his screen. "Naomi said you wanted to see the guest list." He poked at his display. "I'm sending it to you now."

I glanced back at the security video as my wrist vibrated with the incoming message. The big-haired lady was back, sipping champagne. Her hive was unraveling. Connell King was nowhere to be found.

I pulled up the guest list and scanned the names. I recognized a few. Politicians, business tycoons, a few pop celebs. There was only one I knew personally: Ellory Schuyler.

NINE

I left Battle's house and drove down out of the mountains to the coast, where I found a trad-ag diner that promised an ocean view. The view was there if I stood on the banquette to see over the edge of the cliff to the current sloshing inside the seawall. I ordered coffee, eggs and toast. The food came with a side of limpid green melon, a fruit I never could tell if it was trad- or lab-grown. I ate and drank and did some more digging into Battle's party and the client who was actually paying me.

The society sites said nothing about the connection between Battle and Schuyler. There were countless photos from the gala of Battle looking elegant and self-assured in a backless gray dress as she glad-handed one famous guest after another. Schuyler didn't appear in any of those photos, but plenty had been written about him and his company in the past few years. There wasn't anything concrete, but I got the impression everyone believed he was on the backside of his career as a space magnate. Not that I needed a dozen carefully worded profiles to tell me that. At his age, he would be on the backside of everything. It was a fact of life. You learn, you work, you grow old and you die. Nothing lasts. But there was nothing linking him to Battle, other than the recent pieces on Battle winning the Seashell contract. Nothing that gave me additional insight into why Battle would invite a business competitor to a celebratory gala or why Schuyler might have an ulterior motive for hiring me.

The most promising piece was a profile that ran in the *Times* six months ago. It listed Schuyler's career accomplishments and gave him space to reflect on all he had achieved. The journalist then asked Schuyler for his thoughts on the future of space exploration. Schuyler acknowledged the up-and-comers in the field without mentioning Battle or anyone else's names. But he insisted his company would have a say in the next step of humanity's extraterrestrial destiny. "We've been to Mars, but the future is beyond Mars," he said. "At Schuyler Space Industries, we're looking for the right opportunities to extend human civilization into the next centuries, the next millennia."

When I was done reading, I scanned back to the top to find the byline. The journalist's name was Angelina Cho. She could have been a bot, but it would be worth hearing from her either way. I called the *Times's* listed contact, even though the newshub's physical footprint was probably limited to an AI receptionist and a rarely used conference room. No one answered. I sent a message to the paper's main address, asking to speak to Cho, and figured I might get a response in a month—if I was lucky.

Outside the diner, the sun beat down out of an orange-gray sky. Dense green shade trees lined the sidewalk, and there was a slight breeze sweeping down off the mountains and out to the ocean, but none of that did much to cut the midday heat. The street was quiet and empty except for a sleek silver flyer parked behind me and a pair of heavies leaning against my car. They sported matching white skull holoheads in the style of Día de los Muertos icons. Four vertical black lines marked their foreheads. As I approached, they rocked themselves off the car with the controlled ease of men accustomed to overcoming resistance.

"You Carver?" the one on my left asked. He was a tall man with long, thick arms and a high, nasal voice.

"Who's asking?" I said.

"That's him," the other one said. He was a few centimeters taller than me and twice as wide, and his voice matched his figure, echoing around in his barrel chest for a few seconds before he let it out.

"You're coming with us," the tall one said.

"Thanks for the offer," I said, "but I just ate. Let's do dinner instead. Pick me up at seven?" I headed past them, intending to circle around the front of my car to the driver's side.

The stocky man's hand shot out and grabbed me above my left elbow with a grip like a molecular waste compactor. He was quick, but I was quicker. I drew my arm back to absorb the momentum of his grasp, pulling him closer to me as I spun and hit him square in the jaw. He spat, showing a flash of pink before the bared white teeth of his digital face snapped shut again, and laughed. His grip on my arm tightened, and he swung at me with his other hand. I ducked the blow, got a leg behind his, and drove my shoulder into his chest. I moved him a whole centimeter.

The tall man's arms swung down around me from behind, pinning my own limbs to my sides. His partner hit me twice, once in the ribs and once in the temple. I wanted to tell him the first one was enough, that if that was how he really felt, we could have our three-way date then and there. But there wasn't enough time between the two punches and, after the first blow, I didn't have enough air in my lungs to speak. When I managed to lift my head up, two blurry, thick men wavered in front of me. They both leered.

I tried to jump back against the man holding me, but my knees buckled and the arms around me rooted me to the ground. I tried to lift my feet and kick out at where the two men in front of me blended together and succeeding in disturbing a fly hovering around their shared knee before I crashed back to the ground.

A car door slammed.

"That's enough for now," said a voice like a tiger's paw.

The thick man stepped away. The tall man loosened his grip just enough for me to take a shuddering breath. The man who had spoken stepped away from the silver flyer and strode up the pavement toward us. He was smaller than the two goons, but he moved like a featherweight cage fighter.

"Let him go," the featherweight said. "He's smart enough not to try anything."

The tall man unwrapped me. I remembered how to stand on my own two legs before I face-planted on the concrete. I decided to take the bossman's suggestion and play it smart for once. That, and I wasn't sure I had full control of my limbs yet.

Like his two henchmen, the featherweight's holohead was a white skull with four lines on its forehead. It had empty black eyes and a wide mouth studded with pointed teeth. On the top and sides of the skull were the horns, spines and scaly mane of a Chinese dragon, all in white. It would have been terrifying if it wasn't also clear there was a flesh-and-blood man underneath that skull. I had met men like these before. They were everywhere, certainly in every big city. In Chicago, they called themselves the Stone Kings or the Disciples, and they had kept me plenty busy when I was a cop. But I had to give these three credit. Their holoheads were sharp. For three men running around in masks, they had style.

"Do you know who I am?" the featherweight asked.

He was a big man. A man you didn't fuck with if you had any sense. A man who could have had me shot or dismembered or worse and not batted an eye. I said, "You're a man in need of a calendar. It's seven months until Halloween." My head swam, my stomach cartwheeled, and I deposited my lunch at his feet.

The featherweight looked at the splatter of vomit on the ground and laughed. It was a short, hard, cruel laugh. If he watched a baby topple to the ground after taking its first steps, he would probably have laughed like that. "You got guts, Carver," he said. "I'll give you that."

I dredged up what little saliva I could find and spat the acrid taste from my mouth.

"I hear you've been visiting Naomi Battle," he said. "That ends today."

I stood there with my hands on my knees until I was fairly confident my tank was empty. Then I forced myself upright. "I was hired to do a job," I said.

The dragon-skull's black hole eyes threatened to swallow my own. "Did you find anything related to what you were hired to find?"

I didn't answer. The air was a heavy, noxious mixture of brine and smoke, and I was having a hard time breathing.

"Your job is over," the featherweight said. "Take your money and go home." He turned back to his ride.

"What do you want with Battle?" I asked.

He stopped. The two heavies took a step toward me, but he raised a hand to hold them back. "Who said I want anything with Battle?"

I squinted against the sun, which seemed brighter than it was fifteen minutes ago. My temple throbbed where the thick man had hit me. "It's about King, isn't it?"

The featherweight turned to face me. His dragon's teeth came together in a fiendish grin. "The only king around here," he said, "is me."

TEN

There were still a few holdouts who refused to use the autodrive feature in their cars, but when you'd taken a sledgehammer to the ribs and the temple and couldn't walk or see straight, it was a nice amenity to have. I watched the featherweight and his two heavies get into their silver flyer and pull out into the street before ascending up and over the mountains. Then I let the Kwang drive me to the nearest police station while I closed my eyes and waited for the throbbing in my head to subside.

I caught my first murder as a homicide detective a week after Lucia Williams broadcast her killer's message to the city. The victim was a low-level Stone King enforcer named Isaiah Wallace. I didn't have much to go on. Wallace had been stabbed to death, but the murder weapon was never recovered. He had died in the heart of Stone territory, a twenty-square-kilometer zone dubbed the Event Horizon where the Stones had cut off police access to the city's surveillance network. I canvassed the surrounding street for witnesses, but given what happened to Pfenning and Williams, I expected little civilian cooperation over a dead Stone. I wasn't disappointed.

When digital intelligence finally cracked the encryption on Wallace's screen, they found an anonymous message received a week before his death. The sender advertised a $5,000 reward for information on the whereabouts of any known Stones and a $10,000 reward for any Stone body. Three days later, another Stone turned up dead. Two days after that, there were two more bodies. All of them had received the same message on the same date. It had been broadcast to every person within a specific boundary. We suspected a fledgling rival gang was trying to take advantage of the cracks in the Stones' authority. A few cops took to calling this spectral force the Chicago Aazadi, after the Pakistani guerillas harassing troops in Indian-annexed Kashmir. But digital intelligence came up empty when they tried to trace the message back to its source. It takes a lot to get decent people to mark someone for death or carry out an execution themselves. But the Aazadi realized you don't need to turn the decent people. You only need to give the few bad apples a chance to get even more rotten.

Ten days after Wallace's death, the Stones retaliated. The first victim was killed by a single gunshot to the forehead, his body cast in the street, his screen displaying the same message as Lucia Williams's: "SNITCH." Another civilian body was discovered the next day, this one with his eyes carved out. Two more Stone corpses followed the next day, and one Stone and one civilian the day after that. It was clear the Stones were determined to win at any cost. I suspected the same was true of the featherweight in the dragon holohead.

The West LA Station on Santa Monica was an ugly, glimmering box of periwinkle pigmented carbocrete and gleaming mirrored glass. It reminded me of my grandmother's living room sofa with its self-cleaning slip covers. Come on in, tell us all about it, but don't make a mess. Inside, a thick column of convex screens occupied the center of the lobby. A tired old hound dog of a sergeant was speaking with a female citizen on a bench against the front wall. I went to the nearest screen and told a pretty young officer of ambiguous ethnicity all about the bad boys in Halloween masks who had given me a beating.

"I'm very sorry to hear that." The virtual cop's face expressed the appropriate sympathy. "Rest assured, the Los Angeles Police Department shares your concern. An officer will be with you shortly."

A moment later, a cop who shared the thick goon's weight class sauntered into the lobby and led me back to a tinted glass door labeled

Lieutenant Kentavious Washington.

"Mr. Carver!" Washington hailed me as the burly cop held open his door. "One of our own, I hear. Or at least the next best thing." He gestured to the chair facing his desk. "Have a seat."

Washington was shortish and squat with a square, chinless head atop his square body. He had a high forehead and a pelt of close-cropped hair wrapped over his cubic pate. A bristly mustache curled over his upper lip like someone had daubed on a frown in black paint, but his real lips were parted in a shit-eating grin. Next to him stood a tall bruiser with a flat face and crooked nose built like the goon who had given me a hug. And here I thought reproductive cloning was illegal.

"I hear you've run into some trouble," Washington said. "How can I help?"

I described the three toughs in holoheads. Washington listened with an expression of sympathetic concern almost as convincing as the virtual cop's.

When I had finished, his bright, deep-set eyes gave me a once-over. "You ever on the force?" he asked.

"A while back," I said. "In Chicago."

He nodded. "I thought so. I can always spot a man in blue, even out of uniform. But now you've gone private." He leaned back in his chair and spread his arms wide. "Well, we need the help. At least, that's what our governor tells us. And he's got the Supreme Court behind him. So now citizens protect citizens—and the planet, of course—from themselves, with the help of folks like you." He inter-laced his fingers behind his head. "But about those three boys you met. You want me to do what? Arrest them?" He shook his head, and his mustache's frown deepened. "Could be tough. Punks like that do something like you described, the first thing they do after is change their heads."

"I'm wondering if you know who they are," I said.

Washington opened a drawer in his desk and withdrew a glass jar filled with green and white capsules. He tipped one into his palm, swallowed it dry and coughed. Then he held out the jar to me. "Help yourself. It's the latest blend. FDA-approved, non-addictive. Makes you feel like you can bend hebar."

I declined. I didn't need that kind of high, and I preferred to taste my poisons. "They struck me as the type who wear their heads as symbols," I said. "And it was a pretty distinctive design."

"These boys sound familiar to you, Kessler?" Washington asked.

"Like you said, sir, could be anyone under those heads," the flat-faced cop said.

"What about you, Mitchell?"

"No way of knowing," the burly cop behind me echoed.

"Looked like a gang to me," I said. "And not the kind that steals kids' scooters."

Washington shook his head and sighed. "Bad time to visit Los Angeles, what with these fires and all. But they'll burn themselves out sooner or later. They always do." His beady eyes narrowed as he folded his arms atop his desk. "So what brings you to our fair city, Mr. Carver?"

"A case," I said.

"No shit." He massaged his throat. "Who's the client?"

"That's private," I said. "It's in the job title."

Washington smirked. "Fine. Like I said, I know the kinds of cases you boys handle. Do they usually involve gangs? Of any kind?"

"Depends on the case."

"Mm hmm. But you didn't come here to chase around three boys dressed up like skeletons." Washington spoke softly, but his mouth was set in a hard line and the words slithered out like a cornered viper. "That's my job, assuming there's any reason to chase them. Your job is to help whatever do-gooder hired you get themselves a nice payday in court for ratting on their fellow citizen. So I suggest you do your job and let me do mine."

"Just so we understand each other," I said, "you're telling me you know nothing about a gang in this area with holoheads that look like skulls. Is that right?"

"If such a gang exists," Washington said, "we'll take care of it."

"What exactly do you plan to do?" I asked. "If there's no way of knowing who these three are, as you claim."

Washington settled back into his seat and returned the jar of boosters to the drawer. "So you were Chicago PD, huh?"

"That's right."

"And you were what? A beat cop?"

"Detective," I said. "Homicide."

"Detective, huh?" His smarmy grin crept back across his face. "Took quite a tumble, didn't you?"

I let that one flop over and die on his desk.

When I didn't respond, Washington sighed and said, "Well, you know what it's like, anyway. Boys like these, they come and go. But you leave it to us. Like I said, we'll take care of it."

I tried one more time. "A visitor to your city tells you he's been assaulted and threatened by three men, and that's your response?"

Washington slammed both palms onto the surface of his desk and thrust himself to his feet. "My response is that it's none of your goddamn business, Carver!" He stood there, staring down at me for a moment, his chest heaving, then settled back into his chair and wiped his hand down his mouth and neck. When he seemed to have control of himself, he said, "You just do your job and let us do ours."

I crossed one ankle over the other knee and brushed dust off the side of my shoe. "What have you found on the Connell King case?" I asked.

Washington's face went slack. He glanced from Kessler to Mitchell and back to me. "Colonel who?"

"Connell," I said. "King. You know, took a nosedive off the Seventh Street Bridge. Or was pushed. Or thrown. I met one of your detectives on it this morning. He was almost as charming as Kessler here."

Kessler met my gaze, his thumbs hooked into his duty belt. His right palm settled on the butt of his pistol, and the green indicator above the grip lit up as the biometric lock disengaged. His lips curled into a sneer.

"I don't know anything about that," Washington said. "If we've got a detective on it, he'll take care of it. Once again, it's not your concern."

"That's what the dragon-faced guy told me too," I said. "But you wouldn't know anything about that, would you?"

Washington was building up to another explosion, but I spoke first. "Everyone seems very touchy about this Mr. King." I cleaned my other shoe. "You don't have any problem with me visiting Naomi Battle, do you?"

"Naomi ... the rocket lady?" I had to hand it to Washington this time. He looked genuinely perplexed.

"I guess not. Maybe you are different from these skull-heads after all." I stood up. "Well, if I end up with my head blown off, you'll know why. Maybe then you'll look into it."

Washington gave me his fake smile, but his pinpoint eyes and twitchy mustache betrayed his rage. "Thank you for bringing this matter to my attention, Mr. Carver. We'll let you know if we find anything. In the meantime ..."

I headed for the door. Mitchell held it open for me and followed me out into the hallway, close enough that my old shadow filed for unemployment.

The hound dog sergeant intercepted us before we reached the lobby. "I'll take it from here, Mitch," he said.

He grasped my arm in a way that let me know it was just for show and guided me down the hall. He had a tall, weathered face that had taken more than a few beatings and a wide, dented nose. His triangular eyes were taller on the inside edges and narrowed to points on the outsides. They were brown and deep, penetrating, weary and sad. He had dark wavy hair that looked like it never quite obeyed a comb and graying stubble over a once-strong chin that had grown soft with age.

"Keep walking," he said when we were out of Mitchell's earshot. "Don't look at me. I'll answer your questions. But not here. Not now."

"When?" I asked.

The sergeant ushered me through the lobby, past the column of virtual cops and out the front door. Outside, the cloudless sky was hazy and jaundiced, but it was still mid-afternoon and the hard sun blazed down with as much force as it had all day. Across the street, a narrow, peeling white Episcopal church crammed between a dispensary and a two-story police parking lot projected a gaudy and desperate holodisplay reminding everyone that ignoring the will of God was the path to sin and death and advertising upcoming services. The dispensary line wound past the church's closed front door and darkened windows. The holodisplay flickered and died.

"Tonight." The sergeant released my arm. "The Castaway, Santa Monica Pier. Eight o'clock." He re-entered the station, letting the door swing shut behind him without looking back.

ELEVEN

I had planned to spend the first part of the afternoon tracking down Angelina Cho but I didn't have much to go on, and my three new friends in skull masks and the other three who called themselves cops had made me think there was more to learn at Battle's place. I had some questions for Mirlande anyway, and now seemed like the right time to ask them. I considered wearing a holohead and exchanging the Kwang for a different rental before returning to Battle's but decided against it. The three skeletons didn't strike me as the types that were fooled easily. If they wanted me off the screen, I would have to hope I'd see them coming.

But it wasn't the featherweight and his two toughs who stopped me as I ascended the mountain road. Before I reached the rusted metal gate, I found the way blocked by three different, bare-headed figures. I slowed to a stop. Apparently, the two I had seen playing desert scouts the previous morning had found a friend to join them. I rolled down my window as two of them approached, while the third remained planted in the middle of the road.

"You're that private detective here about carbon poisoning," one of them said. I recognized him as the man who'd been creeping along the ridge above me when I saw Mirlande's flyer take off.

"Got any leads?" I asked.

The man planted his hands on the edge of my open window and leaned down to my level. A wave of heat followed him. His long brown hair was tangled and filthy, and his blue eyes glowed piously in his dust- and sun-worn face. "This is our case," he said. "We are California Right to a Future. It's our mission to bring down anyone sullying the air, land and oceans of this state. We don't need your help."

"That's good," I said. "Because I wasn't offering."

He gave me a bishop's sanctimonious, pitying smirk. "You are a mercenary. A hired tool of the system. But carbon poisoning is a crime against humanity and our future. We're here for justice."

"I'm sure your fellow citizens are grateful for your commitment," I said. Dark smoke was rising over the mountains to the north, and I could taste the ashes on the wind. "Even if they're not, some nice fat court settlements should more than make up for it."

"How dare you?" The woman standing behind him took two quick steps forward, her hands balled into fists. "That money is ours by—"

"River." The man cut her off with a raised hand and a pointed look.

She clamped her lips, but her eyes wanted to jump out of her skull and throttle me to death. Despite her name, River also looked as though she had never encountered running water. Her hair was short and ragged, her gaunt cheeks drawn high over a wide nose and protruding jaw. Judging by the state of her and her companions' clothes, they must have been out there for weeks.

The man returned his attention to me. "This is our case," he said. "You're not needed here. You're not welcome here."

"There is no case," I said. "Or hadn't you heard?"

The man stared at me evenly. "We'll be the judge of that," he said finally. But I could tell he wasn't too sure of himself.

"No," I said, "a judge will be the judge of that. Assuming you can even scrape together anything worthy of a lawsuit. But it's a free country, or so they say. I'm not the one who needs a shower and a skin graft."

The man reached down and drew a hatchet from his belt. It

looked authentic enough, with a wood handle and sharpened stone blade. I'd seen pictures of similar weapons in elementary school history textbooks, but I never imagined any still existed in the real world.

"You've been warned," he said. "The next time, there won't be a warning." He whirled, pointed at a gnarled and burned-out tree stump some twenty meters away and cocked his arm to throw.

I reached out and blocked the motion before he could let the weapon fly. "I get the point," I said. "But I have work to do and I don't have time for a show."

I gunned the car forward. The man blocking the road jumped out of the way, evidently forgetting the Kwang's safety system would have engaged the brakes well before it hit him. I left the three self-righteous environmentalists coughing on the dust churned up by my car and continued up the dried-out mountain. Everybody I spoke to wanted me to drop this case. That made me think I was on to something.

I announced myself to the concealed camera, and Mirlande was waiting for me as I pulled into the driveway.

"Welcome back, Mr. Carver," she said as my car drove off. "Any developments with the case?"

"A few," I said. "Actually, I have some questions for you if you can spare the time."

Mirlande stared back at me, her eyes hard and bright. "Now is not the best time, unfortunately. Perhaps—"

"That's okay," I said, "I can wait."

When I didn't move, she said, "Mr. Carver, we are in the middle of a very delicate and— "

"I get it," I said. "You're busy. You don't need to give me all the details. I'm sure they're proprietary, and they would probably go right over my head anyway. Like I said, I can wait."

Mirlande held my gaze, her lips pursed. "All right," she said. "I can give you fifteen minutes. That's it."

"Perfect," I said. "I just have a few questions."

Mirlande led me inside to the elevator. As the car made its brief ascent to the second floor, she faced me with her back straight and chin raised, as though willing herself to grow to my height. "Have you found anything?"

"Some answers," I said. The doors opened and Mirlande led me down the hall. "And more questions."

Mirlande's office looked like a carefully arranged advertisement for iRise. There was a white desk with her computer and white shelves that were mostly empty. The screens on the walls depicted shuttle launches, lunar and Martian terrains, our tiny blue orb in the vast unfeeling blackness of space. On one shelf, a smaller framed screen displayed a photo of Mirlande and Battle at a launch site, arms around each other's shoulders. On her desk was an old hard-copy photo of a man and woman with their hands on the shoulders of a young girl. The girl had Mirlande's eyes and an eager, toothy grin I'd never seen on her face.

Mirlande perched on the edge of her chair and crossed her long, slim legs. "How can I help you, Mr. Carver?"

"What can you tell me about Mr. King?" I asked.

Mirlande's eyes met my gaze, but it was clear she was looking through me. Her jaw- and cheekbones stood out like rail tracks across the sides of her face. "Naomi hired him six years ago. I knew him in a professional capacity, but we didn't interact much."

"Was he good at his job?"

"Yes." Her voice was mechanical and even. "He served in the military, then worked in private security for several years before he came here. He was always well-prepared, meticulous about every detail."

"Did he have a family?"

"An ex-wife and a sister," she said. "No children."

"Have they been notified?"

"Yes," Mirlande said. "When he went missing, I called them to see if they had heard anything. After the police found his body, the detective told us he had notified them."

"You said he had an ex-wife," I said. "He never remarried?"

"No," she said. "Not that I know of."

"What was he like on a personal level?"

Her eyes darted toward the photo on her desk, then back to me. "Why are you really here, Mr. Carver?"

I was there because I didn't know how to leave well enough alone. I was there because unanswered questions grated on my brain like a bad neural implant. I was there because I was chasing the ghost of a long-lost friend. "A man is dead," I said. "The police have known he was missing for two weeks, but they don't seem to have done much about it." From the massive window on the north side of the office, I had an even better view of the billowing wildfire smoke. Every few seconds, a rapidly blooming red mist appeared against the black cloud as a drone released a capsule of supercompressed fire retardant. But these few bright flowers withered in the spreading darkness almost as quickly as they had grown. "So what did you think of Mr. King?"

"Again, I didn't know him that well," Mirlande said. "Like I said, he was good at his job. Very detail-oriented."

"Was he a friendly man?"

Mirlande's lips parted in a narrow oval, but she recovered herself quickly. "Not with me," she answered. "But he wasn't cruel. He was businesslike, I suppose."

"How did your coworkers feel about him?"

"I'm not sure." Her brow furrowed. "Have you talked to them?"

"One or two." I got up and studied a screen showing a still image of the Copernicus Lunar Station. "You didn't confide in each other, share opinions about other coworkers, including Mr. King?" I looked back at Mirlande. "That kind of talk is natural in a workplace, isn't it?"

"I don't know about other workplaces," she said, "but there isn't much gossip here. Or if there is, I'm not usually involved in it."

"Do you know how his marriage ended?" I asked.

"No."

I moved on to a screen displaying the Schiaparelli Base. "What was he like with women in general?"

Mirlande rotated her chair slowly from side to side. "In general? I don't know."

"One of your coworkers told me he could be a little aggressive," I said. "They mentioned some incidents with Ms. Battle's former trainer. I believe her name was Jordan."

"She left about a year ago," Mirlande said. "I heard rumors, but—"

"Rumors?" I turned to face her. "As in gossip?"

Mirlande stopped her chair and met my gaze. "Nothing concrete."

I looked back at the Martian base. "What did you hear?"

"I heard there was some disagreement between the two of them. Eventually, Jordan quit."

"That's all?"

"Yes."

"Ever ask Battle about it?"

"No."

I circled back to my chair and stood behind it with one hand resting on the back. "And King was never aggressive with you?"

Mirlande's fingers curled over the ends of her chair's armrests. "No."

I straightened and moved toward the windows. "The night King disappeared, Battle had a party to celebrate the Seashell contract." Outside, the wind was streaming over the mountaintop and swirling clouds of dust against the house. "Ellory Schuyler was a guest."

I looked over my shoulder. Mirlande was studying me with a furrowed brow and slightly parted lips. "Yes," she said. "He was."

"That wasn't contentious?" I asked. "After all, he and Battle are competitors. I'm sure he wanted that contract as bad as she did."

"He is a competitor." Mirlande sat back, and her hands relaxed into her lap. "But they're also longtime friends."

That was news to me. "So you weren't surprised he was invited? Or that he showed up?"

"No, not at all."

From the driveway, I followed the road down the mountain as far as I could see. River and her friends were nowhere to be found. "Someone left this house in a flyer the first day I was here." I turned to face Mirlande. "Was that you?"

She shrugged. "People leave the house all the time."

I returned to my chair and sat down. "All right. About twenty minutes after I left. That would have been around twelve-fifteen. The flyer headed northeast."

Mirlande pinched her lips into a tight circle. "You seem convinced it was me."

"So tell me a story," I said. "Convince me otherwise." When she said nothing, I asked, "Where did you go?"

"I met a potential investor."

"Where? In their office? Over coffee?"

"East LA," she said. "A public place, but a quiet one. Somewhere that even if anyone saw us, our meeting wouldn't be all over the web in an hour."

"Must have been a big investor." Either Mirlande was lying or iRise's business was shadier than it looked. "I assume you both wore holoheads."

Mirlande angled her head to the side. "It sounds like you were following me, Mr. Carver. Am I a suspect?"

"Everyone's a suspect," I said. "Until they're not."

"Fine," she said. "We wore holoheads."

"How did the meeting go?" I asked. "Did you get the investment?"

"No. Not yet, anyway." Mirlande shifted in her chair and glanced at her screen. "Are we finished here, Mr. Carver? Surely this investor isn't related to Mr. King."

"Yes." I stood up. "I think I've learned everything I can for now."

TWELVE

The Castaway was on the top deck of the dilapidated paddle wheeler that someone had dubbed a pier. It faced southwest, toward the Pacific, though by eight p.m., all that was visible of the ocean were a few waves sloshing in the half-circle illuminated by the deck lights. Inside the restaurant, the furniture was painted in faded and peeling reds, blues, yellows and greens. Dried palm fronds hung around the ceiling perimeter. Drooping brown plants in the corners waited to take their place. Two men sat at opposite ends of the bar. A couple ate in silence at a table in the corner. A man in a loud shirt and a blond-haired, sunburned holohead waved me over to the table where he sat alone.

When I sat down, he extended his hand. "Adrian Moreno."

I shook it. "Marcus Carver."

A cylindrical, white bioplastic robot wheeled over with Moreno's beer on its tray. I ordered one of the same.

"So you got yourself in trouble with the Tongs." Moreno took a drink and wiped the foam from his lip. "I would have advised against that."

"You'd have been the first," I said. "Nobody else on your side seems to know anything about it."

Moreno stared at his beer and ran his thumb through the condensation on the glass. His pensive expression didn't suit his holohead. "I was a Tong once. When I was young and stupid. Maybe that helped me when I got old and less stupid."

The server returned with my beer. I took a drink. It was cold, which was about all it had going for it.

"Sorry," Moreno said. "It's the best they have."

"You know I didn't come for the beer." I took another sip. The heat of the day had lingered past sundown, and my mouth was dry and my head ached. "You said being a former Tong helped you. How so?"

"I hear you were a cop once."

I nodded. "In Chicago."

"Then I'm sure you've seen the same things I did. When you're a kid like I was, you join a gang because you want respect, power, money, the lifestyle. When you're an overworked cop with a few dirty files in your drive, a family to feed and cases you can't crack because you don't understand the latest tech, a little money makes it easy to look the other way. By the time the department catches up, by the time you understand who you're really dealing with, it's too late."

"Washington," I said.

Moreno shook his head and sighed. "Washington is a mediocre cop who got a few promotions and realized he enjoyed giving orders more than taking them. But he's just one of many the Tongs have compromised."

I got it. I had worked under a sergeant like Washington back in Chicago, though I never had reason to believe he was anything more than incompetent. "So what's their racket?" I asked, though based on my experiences with the Stone Kings, I was pretty sure I already knew.

"The only vice that's left," Moreno said. "Information. Forging identities, selling secrets, hacking, blackmail—plus whatever it takes to protect that business."

It was the same thing in Chicago, I told Moreno. When you never knew who was watching and the wrong secret could cost you your reputation, life's savings or freedom, guarding and exposing that kind of info was priceless.

He nodded. "As far as I know, the shift started on the west coast.

The Chinese gangs were the first to make the jump, and when the drug trade dried up, the Latino crews followed suit. But I hear it's everywhere now." He took another drink. "Tell me about these three you met."

I described the three men and their holoheads.

Moreno whistled softly. "I don't know about the first two, but the third sounds like Yuze Enriquez. Chief Tong himself. No one I know has ever seen his real face, but that's his holohead."

"I must have really struck a nerve," I said.

Moreno grinned. "From what I heard in Washington's office, that probably wasn't the first time. Seems like you have a certain way with people." He looked up at the baseball game playing on a screen on the wall to our right. "I used to love the Dodgers," he said. "Still do, I guess. But I rarely watch anymore. I'm old enough to remember when the jerseys were all white and blue, when peds were still banned. It seemed like a different game then. But it probably wasn't. I was just seeing it with different eyes."

He turned back to me and leaned forward, crossing his arms and resting his forearms on the table. "Tell me about yourself, Mr. Carver."

"Marcus," I said. "Or Carver. I don't care which. There's not much to tell. I'm thirty-three years old. Born on the south side of Chicago and lived there my whole life. I graduated from college only because my pops wouldn't let me leave after two years to become a cop. I like women, but I've never found one who made me regret being a bachelor. I was a cop for a while, a detective for most of it, and now I'm private."

"You ever do anything else for a living?" Moreno asked.

"No."

"Me either. Not counting my Tong days."

I had met a few cops like Moreno too, though they seemed to be outnumbered by the Washingtons. It was easy to say you cared about justice, about protecting the innocent. But after you'd spent some time on the streets, the lines between villain and hero, corrupt and innocent, tended to blur together. Many cops soon realized they enjoyed some extra green and a bit of power a lot more than justice.

"Any idea why Enriquez cares so much about Naomi Battle?" I asked.

Moreno shrugged. "Specifics? No. In general, I think you can figure that out."

"She has something they want," I said. "Information, money, maybe both."

"That's it." Moreno's hand circled his half-empty glass, but he didn't lift it off the table. "I haven't crossed Enriquez much. But from what I've heard, once he gets his phishhooks in, he doesn't let go." He jutted his chin at me. "Why do you care so much about Battle?"

"I was hired to investigate her on another matter," I said. "The day after I show up, an LAPD detective stops by to tell Battle her security captain took a header off a bridge. Then three gangsters in skeleton masks warn me off. Later on, a trio of greenies in dirty desert fatigues do the same. Maybe they're all coincidences. But I never believed in coincidences."

"What's this other matter?" Moreno asked.

"That's between me and my client."

"If it's linked to a murder—"

"It's civil. Not your territory."

"Combustion."

I didn't answer.

Moreno exhaled slowly. "Hard way to make a living," he said. "Those laws—"

"Save it," I said. "I've heard it all before."

He held my gaze. "I bet you have."

The room around us was quiet. No one appeared to be listening to our conversation, but they also didn't seem happy to be there. One of the two at the green-painted bar had left. The other sat on a red stool with his back to us, his forearms resting on the bar, one arm moving robotically every minute or so to raise his drink to his lips. The couple in holoheads at the blue table in the corner mumbled an occasional word to each other while staring at their plates but scarcely lifted their heads to look into their partner's digital eyes. A newcomer in a green chair at a red table across the room was staring into space or at the projection from his screen.

"What have you found on Connell King?" I asked Moreno.

"King?"

"Battle's security man."

"It's not my case," he said. "Even if it was—"

"You couldn't tell me," I finished. "That didn't stop you from telling me about Enriquez and his crew."

"That's different."

"Maybe so. How's this? Has the ME's report come back yet?"

Moreno scowled at me but tapped his screen. His eyes held mine as he scrolled through his concealed display.

"I've got two guesses." I watched Moreno's finger swipe the air. "You tell me if I'm wrong. One, King died long before his body was discovered. Almost two weeks earlier." Moreno glanced up at me but said nothing. "Two, the ME found traces of biological materials on his clothing. Dirt, plant material, pollen. The kind of stuff that doesn't get plastered to you by slamming into carbocrete."

Moreno's hand dropped to the table, and his eyes narrowed. It was another odd expression for his red-cheeked tourist holohead.

"Any footage from the bridge?" I asked.

"No."

Of course not. The Stones wouldn't have left any traces either.

Moreno swiped his display closed. "What do you know?"

"King didn't die at the bridge," I said. "He died at Battle's house."

"How?"

"I don't know for sure. Not yet anyway. And I don't want you to go around making wild accusations." I cracked a smile. "That's my department. But if I find out something definite, you'll be the first to know."

Moreno shook his head. "I hope you're as good as you think you are, Carver. Because if you're not, you're a real pain in the ass."

"And you're an honest cop who can't afford to be wrong," I said. "Especially not on someone with Battle's profile."

"You forgot devilishly handsome," Moreno said.

I decided I liked Moreno. "I try to be honest too. It's a rare thing in this world."

Moreno laughed. "I'll give you a day. Then I want to know what you know, or what you think you know."

I liked his offer a lot more than Schuyler's. "Deal."

Moreno glanced down at his screen, and his face darkened. "Here's another coincidence for you, and you're not going to like it any more than the others. Someone called in a homicide. It's at Battle's place."

THIRTEEN

I scanned the table code and paid our tab. "I've paid more for worse information," I told Moreno when he tried to argue. "If you're still upset, you can turn on your lights and give me an escort to Battle's."

He laughed. "You looking for protection?"

"What can I say?" I replied. "If I'm dead, who's going to spend the money I'm making for this job?"

"All right," he said. "You can follow me. But if anyone asks, you went there on your own."

The drive back along the coast seemed to take forever. Beyond the whisper of the Kwang's engine and the rush of the occasional passing car, I could just make out the murmur of the waves as they left their trace on the curving glass wall. Ahead of me, Moreno's lights illuminated the legs of water running down the panes in swirling beams of blue and white. We swept up into the foothills, past the gaily lit houses that shone even whiter in the dark, then curved around the black and twisting passes into the mountains.

As we pulled into Battle's driveway, a new detective was canvassing the scene. A pair of CSIs were already circling the corpse. By the time I stepped out of my car, I knew exactly who the victim was by the location of her body.

The detective nodded somberly at Moreno as we approached. "Hey Sarge." She glanced at his brightly colored shirt. "Nice threads."

Moreno inclined his head at the mounded sheet lying in the dirt next to the low wall on the west side of Battle's house. "Who is it?"

"Her name is Camila Giménez." The detective gestured at the mansion looming over us. "She was Naomi Battle's personal chef."

At the edge of the sheet, a black pool glimmered in the light from Battle's house. I stood next to it and tried not to see Julia Noi lying there. It didn't work. I saw her in every dead body I'd come across since hers.

My first memory of Julia was looking up at her from flat on my back after she almost took my chin off during the final match of an Academy combat tournament. She was a broad-shouldered woman with a square jaw, crooked nose and carbon-black hair pulled into tight braids that circled her scalp like a crown. I thought I saw a few hairs out of place as she looked down at me. I felt my face to see if it was still intact and tried to console myself with the thought that I had at least made her work a little.

Julia extended a hand to me. I took it, and she dragged me to my feet. Her hard, flinty eyes softened, and her lips parted around her mouthguard.

"You need to move your head more," she said. "You're an easy target."

At the moment, my head felt like it was moving too much. "That should be easier next time." I rubbed my throbbing jaw. "I think you loosened it up for me."

Julia arched a narrow ebony eyebrow. "Next time?"

I pulled out my mouthguard and worked my chin around. Everything seemed to be in place. "Maybe in a week or two."

Julia took me up on my offer. We sparred every week during our time at the Academy. I almost beat her once. Now she was gone, and so was Camila.

From far away, I heard Moreno speaking to the detective. "What happened?"

"Gunshot to the right side of the head," the detective said. "Small caliber projectile. Looks like a drone shot."

Moreno stared up at the night sky. "Battle doesn't have a dome?"

I remembered the buzz of the electrified perimeter fence.

"She does," the detective said.

"But it was down," Moreno said.

She nodded.

I drifted away and headed toward the house. In the entry hall, Battle was conferring with a tall, slender woman who looked like a runway model, but Mirlande intercepted me before I could close the front door.

Her eyes were bloodshot, and her face was drawn and gray. "It's Camila," she said. "Camila ..." She twisted her hands together, folded them, let them fall loose at her sides. "I can't believe it. She didn't ... she was a good ... how could anyone do that to her?"

I took Mirlande by the arm and guided her out to the courtyard. "Let's sit down," I said.

She sank into one of the reclining lounge chairs surrounding the pool, shivering even though the night air was still warm. I sat down in the chair next to her and rested my forearms on my thighs.

"When did this happen?" I asked.

"About an hour ago." Mirlande's teeth chattered as she spoke.

I took the neatly folded towels off our chairs and draped them over her. "Who found her?"

"Dev." She pulled the towels snug around her shoulders. "The new security chief. He said he saw her on one of the cameras. She was lying on the ground on the west side of the house. When he went out to look, she was ..." Her body shook with a heavy sob.

I reached out and squeezed her shoulder. She took a few deep, shuddering breaths. I imagined Camila sipping her tequila and looking out over the darkened valley after a long day of work. If the detective was right, she hadn't even seen it coming.

"Did Dev see anyone else out there?" I asked. It was a false hope, but I preferred to deal with flesh-and-blood assassins over machines.

"I don't know."

"Was anyone else in the house hurt?"

"I don't think so."

"You saw Dev come back inside?"

"Yes. He told Naomi what happened." She stared up at the starless night sky.

"Mirlande," I said. "Look at me."

She pulled the towels tighter and turned her head slowly in my direction.

"This is important," I said. "Do you know why anyone would want to hurt Camila?"

She glanced at me and shivered. Then she began to cry, softly at first, her chin tucked to her chest, then in great heaving sobs that caused her head to bob between her body's tremors.

"Mirlande," I said, "if you know anything ..."

But she shook her head and went on sobbing. I stood and walked a few meters away, where I waited with my back turned and listened as her cries gradually subsided. When she was quiet, I turned back to her, but she stood and pushed past me, breaking into a choppy run as she neared the house and flung open the door. I followed, watching through the window as she shook free from Battle's embrace and hurried to the elevator.

Battle approached me as I re-entered the house. It was the only time I ever saw her looking less than perfectly assured. Her eyes were red, her face drawn, her shoulders, if not slumped, at least slightly relaxed from her usual military posture. She glanced at the elevator doors that had just closed behind Mirlande. "We're all pretty shaken up."

I stood there in the immaculate pink- and black-tiled entryway of a mansion that was supposed to be a safeguard against this kind of tragedy. "I can imagine."

Battle shook her head, her eyes unfocused. "First Connell, and now Camila. I can't believe it."

"What do the police say?"

Battle looked back at me. "Nothing. Platitudes." Her eyes were bright but had not yet recovered their usual fire. "They'll let me know if they find anything."

The runway model walked over to us. Battle shook off my gaze and rested a hand on the other woman's lower back. "This is my partner, Chantal Boldin."

Boldin extended her hand. I shook it and introduced myself. Her grip was like a nanosilk glove, her face as smooth and symmetrical as well-rolled dough, with only the scarcest cracks to betray any aging.

"It's horrible," Boldin said. "We just saw her. She served us dinner. She walked back into the kitchen. And now she's gone."

I stared at her as her words swirled and settled in my brain. She gave me a tight, courteous smile with more stopping power than a railgun. Another second or two and she would have dropped the courtesy.

"So what do you think?" Battle asked.

"Huh?" I tore my gaze away from Boldin.

"What do you think about Camila?" Battle said. "About all of this?"

"I think somebody has found a reason to target you or your company." I pointed at the ceiling. "Is Dev still working?"

"He is." Battle's eyebrows knitted together. "I'll take you up."

When the elevator doors had closed behind us, Battle said, "While you're here, would you mind looking at something?" She showed me her screen. "This was sent to me on April eleventh from an anonymous account. Does it mean anything to you?"

"I know what you did," the message said. "The cops may have missed it, but I saw everything. You have three days to come clean. Confess your crime to the police and the world. If you don't, I'll ruin you."

I looked at Battle. "Does it mean anything to you?"

She shook her head. "Nothing whatsoever."

"Then it may be unrelated to all of this." The elevator doors opened, and we headed down the hallway. "But take a look at your accounts just in case. Business and personal. Have your accountant do it if you don't find anything, and let me know if anything looks off."

"You think whoever sent this hacked my accounts?" she asked.

"I don't know. 'I'll ruin you' could mean revealing whatever secret they think they have on you. Or it could mean ruining you financially."

"All right," she said. "I'll let you know what I find."

When we got to his office, Dev Chaudhri was leaning over his desk, his hands whizzing across his computer display.

"I don't know what happened," he said when Battle left us. "The security system went down for a second, then went right back on. I checked all the cameras, and that's when I saw her, face-down on the ground."

"A hack?" I asked.

"That's the only thing I can think of," Chaudhri said. "But that's not possible without—"

"Someone on the inside," I finished.

He nodded. "Even then, whoever did it would have to be a fucking wizard."

"If there was a breach, can you close it?"

"Already did that," he said. "At least, I think I did."

"Do you still have the footage from the night of the party?" I asked. "The one we looked at the last time I was here."

He stared at me like I'd asked him for footage of the Bering Wind Farm. "Sure. But why?"

"Indulge me."

He pulled it up, and I watched it through once, then a second time to make sure.

"Stop there." I pointed at the display. "Eight thirty-seven p.m. Can you show me the other balconies at this exact moment?"

Chaudhri pulled up the feeds.

"All right," I said. "Thanks. That's all I needed to see."

I left Chaudhri staring after me with his mouth hanging open and returned to the first floor. As I came out of the elevator, I saw Mirlande heading toward the front door.

Battle broke away from a conversation with Boldin, Moreno and the detective. "Did you find what you were looking for?"

"Yes," I said. "Just one more thing: Mirlande told me you consider Ellory Schuyler a friend. Is that true?"

"Ellory?" Battle's face softened. "Yes. A mentor, really. He taught me a lot when I first entered the industry. Why?"

I shrugged. "I figured he was your rival. I guess I was wrong."

Mirlande exited, closing the front door behind her.

"I'll be in touch," I said to Battle.

I left the house in time to see a car heading out of the driveway and down the mountain. I jumped into my own car and sped after it.

FOURTEEN

Mirlande's car had passed the security fence by the time I caught up with her. There was barely room for two cars on the winding mountain road, but I screwed my eyes to the dusty path, swung out to the cliff side and banked in front of her. Her car skidded to a stop a half-meter short of my passenger door. I got out and walked to her vehicle. She stared at me sullenly for a minute before she unlocked the door.

I lowered myself into the passenger seat. "I'm sorry about Camila," I said. "I only spoke to her once, but she seemed like a good woman."

Mirlande gazed at her hands clutching the steering wheel. "She was," she whispered.

"You didn't kill her," I said.

You didn't kill me, I heard Julia say.

Not now, I told her silently.

Mirlande rested her forehead on her hands. Her forearms tightened as she clenched the wheel.

"I can help you," I said.

You can't help me, Julia said.

I know. I gave my head a quick, firm shake, and Julia receded into my memories.

Mirlande laughed, a hard, bitter sound that died as quickly as it began. "Camila's dead. It's too late."

"I can't help her," I said. "But there's still hope for you." I turned to face her, my back against the passenger door. "Let's go back to Connell King."

"King?" She wheeled on me, eyes red-rimmed and blazing like a pair of suns. "King's dead too. The police still don't know who killed him." She was screaming now. "No one does."

"That's easy," I said. "You did. Or at least you helped him to his death."

Mirlande stared at me, eyes bulging, jaw locked, skin taut across her face. Then she said, "How dare you? Two people are dead, and you—"

"Save it," I said. "It's all on the security tapes from the party. The cops and Dev were looking at everything and saw nothing. But when I saw you, I knew what to look for. King went out to the balcony, wearing a holohead. You were already there, and you were the only one who came back."

Mirlande's tightly drawn face collapsed. "I didn't ... He ..."

"I know his reputation. He'd been after you for a while, hadn't he?"

She nodded. "Weeks."

"That night at the party, he had too much to drink. He saw you alone on the balcony and cornered you. And when he made his move ..."

Mirlande glanced away. "I stepped aside. He reached for me, and I stepped aside. I don't know if I pushed him too. Maybe I did. I've tried to remember the truth these last two weeks. I go to sleep every night having convinced myself it was his own momentum that took him over the edge. I wake up every morning after one long nightmare in which I push him over and over again."

"It doesn't matter," I said. "Not really. He attacked you, you defended yourself. What matters is what you did next."

Mirlande leaned her head back against her seat, her hands squeezing her upper arms, her feverishly bright eyes staring straight ahead.

My screen lit up with a message from Battle: "Something's off in the iRise corporate account. I'm having my accountant look into it."

I dismissed the message and turned my attention back to Mirlande. "Everything changed when you found out I didn't work for CSB. And when I started sniffing around that balcony, you thought I was on to you."

Mirlande gazed out over the darkened valley, and her voice drifted to me from across that darkened expanse. "After it happened, I waited for an eternity on that balcony. I was sure someone had seen what had happened, had heard King scream as he went over. But no one came. When they finally did, they weren't there to arrest me. They were talking, laughing. They didn't know what had happened. They didn't even care that I was there. So I went inside. I thought I would tell the first person I recognized. Not that I wanted to. I just felt like I couldn't hold on to that weight. But no one noticed me. When I came in, the band kept on playing, the guests kept on talking and drinking and dancing. I wandered around the ballroom, searching for anyone I knew. With every step, the whole thing felt more unreal. When I finally found Naomi, she smiled and handed me a glass of champagne. I didn't say a word. It was like it had never happened.

"Over the next few days, I was sure I would be found out. Someone would see the video. Someone would find the body. Then the police came and went, and they didn't find anything either. Days passed. A week. You showed up. I think if I had known you were a detective from the start, I would have led you around the house with an empty grin and a few pleasantries. I would have played the innocent host, even though I would have almost hoped you had found something, just so the nightmare would be over. But the way it happened, the shock that you weren't who you said you were—I hadn't prepared for that. I expected an arrest, trial, prison. Instead, it felt like you were toying with me."

I said, "So you decided you needed help, and you knew people who could make the whole thing disappear. Make it look like King died somewhere else."

"He's the cousin of one of my best friends." She glanced at me and looked away. "Ostin Torres. I met him a few times. My friend told me stories. I don't know how true they were. But I thought he could help. I thought it would be easy, merely a matter of money. I'm well-paid, and I would have given almost anything to put the whole thing behind me."

"But it wasn't easy," I said. "When the Tongs found out who you were, who you worked for …"

She rubbed her arms as if still cold. "I don't know if it was Ostin who made the decision or someone else. But it was Ostin who told me what I had to do."

"Help them hack iRise's accounts."

"He said it would be simple. That all I had to do was authenticate the first breach, and that would be enough. He said they would cover their tracks and only pull a little at a time."

"And you agreed."

"Not at first. I told him I would pay them out of my own pocket, if that's what they wanted. I tried to back out. The next call was from someone I didn't know. He threatened to pin King's death on me. He said they could produce a video that showed me pushing him. I didn't know if it was true. But I couldn't take that chance."

We were out of sight of Battle's house, and the night was black and still, save for the faint glow of the fires to the north. The dim interior lights of the car seemed dazzling by comparison. Our reflections in the windows obscured most of the outside world, and it wasn't hard to imagine we were drifting alone upon some vast, empty sea.

"You never thought to go to Battle?" I asked. "Not when King started harassing you? Not after he died?"

Mirlande's gaze flashed to me. "Of course I did. But I couldn't be sure how far she'd go. I thought I could hold off King long enough that he'd lose interest. I didn't want to ruin everything I'd worked for, everything we'd accomplished. If anyone outside of iRise ever learned about what happened to him … It would be my image against his. A black woman against a white man. You understand. All I have is my word. America may have come a long way in the last century, but I still didn't like my odds." She turned away and dug her fingers into her arms. "I was born in Haiti. A hurricane destroyed my family's home when I was eight. My mother and I came to America after that. Two years later, my mother was deported. The next hurricane killed her and my father. I'm where I'm meant to be. I'm not going back."

"I'm sorry," I said. "About your parents."

She mumbled what might have been a thank you. The car's interior lights dimmed. Being a detective meant working back in time. The Earth continued its inexorable rotation from darkness to light to dark, indifferent to the atrocities of humankind, and I worked in the other direction, turning back the days until I could see the suspect and their motive. And while I spun my way back to Battle's party and King's demise, Mirlande's orbit had continued forward, engulfing others as it went, so that even now, sitting half a meter apart in her car; we were slipping past each other in opposite directions, like two planets in retrograde.

"So you did it," I said. "You helped the Tongs hack Battle and iRise."

Mirlande nodded and continued to stare out the window.

"Do you want to tell me what happened next?" I asked. "Or should I guess?"

"It doesn't matter." She sank farther into her seat, her head bowed. "You seem to know it all already."

"Everyone got what they wanted," I said. "At least at first. The Tongs began pulling money, and they moved King to make it look like he was killed somewhere else. But you felt guilty. The police had King's body, so it would be harder for the Tongs to make it look like you killed him here. You closed off access to the accounts. But the Tongs had penetrated everything, including security. When they saw you had shut off the accounts, they threatened to kill someone close to you, close to Battle, unless you reopened the channel."

Mirlande's wiry frame shook once, twice, with silent sobs. Then she drew herself upward, clasped her hands in her lap and held herself still. "Camila."

"It wasn't your fault," I said. "You got involved with the wrong people, but you didn't kill her."

"I might as well have."

"But you didn't," I repeated. "The Tongs did."

She exhaled slowly. I couldn't tell whether she had resigned herself to the truth or was mustering some desperate strength. "What happens now?" she asked.

"We should go back," I said.

Mirlande nodded but didn't start the car. "Why are you here?" she asked. "Who hired you?"

"I'm a private detective," I said. "But I wasn't hired to investigate King."

"So it was a coincidence?"

I remembered what I had told Moreno about coincidences. "Maybe. Maybe not."

Mirlande shifted her body sideways to lean against her door. "What were you looking for?"

I met her gaze. "People hire me in confidence. I know that means nothing to most people, but it means something to me. Who they are, what they want me to do, that's between me and my clients."

"You were snooping around the electrical and climate systems." Her eyes narrowed. "Tapping the walls, feeling behind furniture. You were looking for a combustion violation."

"You angling for my job?"

"That's it, isn't it? You're one of those detectives someone hires to find evidence for a lawsuit."

I stared back at her in silence.

"So your job is to discover people's private secrets and sell them for money." She gave another bitter laugh. "You're no better than the Tongs."

I knew she was only half-wrong. I didn't feel great about bluffing my way into Battle's home and scouring it from top to bottom. I didn't feel great about a lot of the things I did in this job. But I wasn't a cop anymore and probably never would be again, and I could stomach this work a lot better than working as a defense investigator for Nathan Hayes. I said, "I didn't kill Camila. I didn't steal from Battle. And you may not like it, but I have the law on my side."

Mirlande started to respond, but something outside the car caught her attention. There was a sharp thud below me, followed by a slow hiss.

"Get down!" I pulled Mirlande against me.

A shadow flitted past my window, and the car lurched forward.

FIFTEEN

The shadow darted to the back of the car. The thud and hiss repeated themselves. The car tipped to the passenger side. A dirt-smudged face appeared in my window.

"Get out," the hatchet-wielding Right to a Future leader said.

I let go of Mirlande. Her eyes widened as she stared at the face in the glass. "What the hell?"

Behind Mirlande, River peered in through the driver's side window.

"I'm pretty comfortable here, thanks," I shouted to the man.

"Who are they?" Mirlande asked.

"California Right to a Future," I said. "They're like me, but with better uniforms."

The leader smashed his hatchet against my window. The first blow produced a spider's web of cracks in the glass. The second sprayed tiny shards across my face. I pushed my shoulder against the car door and shoved it open into him. It was enough to drive him back a few steps and allow me to get out in a less vulnerable position. I closed the door behind me as the leader regained his footing. He lunged forward and shoved the hatchet handle up under my chin. He was trying to pin me up against the car, but I had given myself enough space to twist away and hit him with a right across the side of his face. At the same time, I got my left hand up to the hatchet and wrenched it away from him as he fell against the hood of the car. River slid across the hood to our side, but I kicked her feet out from under her as soon as she landed. She bounced off the car and rolled into the dust. By the time she got to a knee, I had the man by his loose, dirty hair with the hatchet blade under his chin.

"Back up," I said. "Your friend here could use a shave, but it's dark and my hand's not too steady."

Her eyes blazed in the night, but she took two steps back and waited there, poised to strike.

"Where's the third one of you?" I asked.

Neither answered. The night wind was acrid and dry, and I could taste the grit in the air. I slapped the leader with the flat of the hatchet. He howled and tried to roll away, but I had a firm grip on his tangled locks. River's eyes flicked to the back of the car. I took a quick glance in that direction and saw another shadow behind the rear driver's side.

"Come out," I yelled. I pressed the hatchet against the leader's throat. "Tell him."

"Do it," he said.

The other man edged around the car. I could see he was looking for an opening, but I held the hatchet firmly against his leader's neck. For all their posturing, I could tell these three had never found themselves in a position like this one.

When the other man had circled to the front of the car, I ordered him to stand next to River. He obeyed, but he wasn't happy about it.

"Here's what's going to happen," I said. "You two are going to take a seat over there against the mountain. Do that now." River and the other man shuffled back and lowered themselves to the ground. "My friend here is going to get in my car and turn it around."

I raised my chin toward Mirlande, who had climbed out of her car once I had the three Futurists under control. I sent the key to her screen, and she executed a careful five-point turn on the narrow road.

"Now you and I are going to take a ride," I said to the leader. I hauled him up and walked him in front of me to my car. "You two stay right there," I told the others. I pushed the leader into the back seat and got in after him without breaking contact between the hatchet blade and his throat.

"Take us back to the house," I said to Mirlande.

She looked at me in the rearview mirror, eyes wide and lips parted, but then drove slowly up the incline.

"What's your name?" I asked the leader.

His Adam's apple bobbed under the hatchet. "Todd."

I fought back a snide comment and said, "All right, Todd. We're going to drop my friend off, and then I'll let you go. Don't do anything we'll both regret, and this will all be over soon."

The chain-link fence opened as Mirlande approached. I thought I heard the hum of electricity, but maybe that was just wishful thinking.

"You're dropping me off?" she asked. "What am I supposed to do?"

"Nothing," I said. "Stay out of sight. The Tongs may have drones."

Mirlande turned to look at me. The car drifted slightly toward the cliff.

"Keep your eyes on the road," I said as calmly as I could manage.

"What about Naomi?"

Todd squirmed in the seat next to me. I yanked his hair taut, and he groaned and froze.

"What about her?" I said. "Tell her whatever you want. But she has a high-priced security system and every motivation to keep her employees safe." I could only hope Chaudhri had regained control of that system. "There aren't a lot of good options right now, but her house is the least risky."

Her eyes flashed to the rearview mirror and returned to the road. "I could go with you."

"And do what? The only way this stops is if we bring down the Tongs." Todd shifted again, but I made sure he wasn't going anywhere. "If you want to make things right, pull together a record of everything that happened. Names, dates, times, login records. Any hard copies of communications. All transactions from the accounts. The more detailed, the better."

Her gaze was fixed straight ahead, and her hands clenched the wheel. When we pulled into the driveway, she sat there without moving.

"Go inside," I told her. "Stay there."

"I can't—" she began.

"You can," I said. "They got Camila when she came outside. I'm going to do what I can to crack this, but it won't matter if the Tongs get to you first. So let Dev know what's up, stay inside the house, and keep away from the windows."

She turned around in her seat to look at me. "What are you going to do?"

"I'm going to return this clown to his friends, and then I'm going to figure out how to fight back." I sent her Moreno's details. "If you see anything suspicious, call him. But don't go anywhere."

She glanced from me to Todd. "Be ... Don't do anything stupid."

"I can't promise that," I said. "But I have no interest in getting myself killed. Now go."

She slid out of her seat and walked to the house, stopping before she went inside to look back at the car. I wondered if she was thinking the same thing I was, that this might be the last time we'd ever see each other.

But the hatchet in one hand and Todd's hair in the other brought me swiftly back to the moment. I pushed him forward. "Get up front and drive us back to your friends."

I kept the hatchet on him the whole time, but the short ride passed without incident. We found the other two greenies arguing in the middle of the road, but they stopped when we pulled up next to them.

"Like I said the last time we met, there is no combustion case," I told Todd. "Your work here is done. I'm keeping this hatchet as payment for the two tires you slashed. I suggest you go back to where you came from and find somewhere else to play spies. If you choose to ignore me and keep snooping around this mountain, the least you can do is keep anyone else away from the house." I leaned between the two front seats. "Open the door." He did. "Now get out." He went.

I climbed into the driver's seat and locked the door behind him. Then I eased my car past Mirlande's and headed back down the mountain and into the night.

SIXTEEN

I sent a message to Moreno telling him what I knew. Ten minutes later, he replied with an address and told me to meet him there as soon as possible. I let the Kwang drive, and as it circled north around Battle and Schuyler's ridges, the wildfires flared up ahead of me. Even at that distance, I could scarcely tear my eyes away from the orange flames lapping up the dried-out mountain forests. The Kwang exited the freeway and headed west, and I watched the fires light up the night until they slipped away behind me. Nothing lasts, but some things blaze a little brighter before they too are consigned to ash.

The Kwang stopped in front of a boulder formation in a dusty plot of land on the edge of Encino. I had to go around to the far side of the rocks before I spotted the dim band of light emanating from the base of the formation. I eased the car forward and down a steep driveway that plunged below the boulders and into the earth. A corrugated black gate closed over the entrance behind me. About ten meters down, the incline leveled out, and I parked in front of what looked like an oversized shipping container made from hempcrete and mass timber. Moreno was leaning against his car, waiting for me. He led me up the front path, between a long mirrored window and a sprawling acacia growing out of a carefully groomed plot of sand and creosote bushes. He knocked softly on the door. A woman in a wheelchair opened it almost immediately.

She nodded at Moreno. "Good evening, Sergeant."

Moreno cocked his head back at me. "Assistant District Attorney Hana Yee, meet Private Investigator Marcus Carver."

"A pleasure, I'm sure." Yee turned and wheeled into the house. "Come in, both of you. Lock the door behind you."

We followed Yee into an orderly, spacious kitchen with tiered counters and a single can light above the island providing the sole illumination. A broad window looked out on a neat backyard of crushed pebbles surrounding a pool and jacuzzi, both of them modest compared to Battle's. The water shimmered in the sparse artificial light of Yee's subterranean cave.

Yee pushed her chair to a lower section of the island. Her clothes looked loose enough to accommodate an exoskeleton, but I could understand not wanting to change yourself to cater to others' expectations. She indicated the surrounding bar stools. "Have a seat."

She was a slight woman with a round face and short black hair. Her heavy, dimpled cheeks contributed to her tired, haggard look. Yet I didn't get the impression that we had dragged her out of bed for this meeting. Moreno was a tired-looking cop. Hana Yee looked like she hadn't slept in days and was determined to never do so again. Evidently sleeplessness was the sign of a conscience.

"Can I offer you anything?" She pointed to the counter on her right. "There's coffee if you want it." She withdrew a short, graduated, glass straw and a tin the size of a tablespoon from her pocket. She opened the tin, dipped the straw into the white powder inside, and capped the end with her finger. "I'd offer you some of this, but you probably wouldn't like it. It's a custom blend, and there's not much of a high." She brought the straw to her nose and snorted the powder.

I helped myself to some coffee.

Moreno shook his head when I held the pot up to him. "Never got the fix."

Yee rubbed her nose and pocketed her tin of drugs, and I sat back down and took a sip of mine.

"So, Mr. Carver." Yee sniffed and fixed me with her bright, alert eyes. "I hear you have a case against the Tong Syndicate."

I glanced at Moreno. He had turned off his holohead, and his mournful hound dog gaze was steady and earnest. "She's on our side," he said.

I told Yee what I had discovered, about my run-in with Enriquez and his Tong heavies, and what Mirlande had confessed to me.

As I spoke, she wheeled to the sink, rinsed out her straw and shook it dry. Then she returned to her original place on the island and twirled the straw between her first two fingers. When I had finished, she said, "That's one way of looking at it."

"It is," I said. "What's yours?"

"Ms. Joseph killed King, who was head of security to one of the richest people in this state." The straw stopped and pointed at me. "With him out of the way, it was easier for her to partner with the Tongs to hack Battle's accounts."

I glanced from Moreno to Yee and shook my head. "That doesn't fit. If Mirlande killed King to facilitate access to the iRise accounts, why wait two weeks for the hack?"

She shrugged one shoulder. "To let the police investigation die down."

"Then why go to the Tongs after I showed up?"

"She didn't know you were a detective at first. Only that you weren't an electrician. There are several plausible explanations." She enumerated them with her fingers as she spoke. "Maybe she thought you were trying to beat the Tongs to the hack. Maybe she thought you were a Tong and wanted them to back off. Maybe she simply got nervous that someone was snooping around Battle's."

"So then what? The Tongs hack Battle. Giménez gets in the way, and they kill her?"

Yee pressed both palms down toward the counter. "Please keep it down," she said. "My kids are sleeping." She flipped her hands over, fingers splayed, and angled her head to the side. "As for Giménez, sure, why not?"

I kept my voice neutral. "Come on. Battle's personal chef has a hand in cybersecurity? The Tongs should have killed Chaudhri. And another thing, why move King's body? Either Mirlande thought I was angling for the same score, in which case King could stay where he was. Or she suspected I was investigating his death, in which case she would have waited for the investigation to die down the same as she did after the police first showed up. Not to mention the fact that this entire supposed scheme depends on having an untrained civilian off an ex-soldier while the Tongs have professional killers sitting around fiddling with their screens."

Yee smirked. "You got a thing for this girl, don't you?"

"Sure," I said. "But she wouldn't be the first pretty woman I've put away. Either way, if we agree the Tongs hacked Battle and killed Giménez, we can bring them all in and sort out what's what."

Yee rested one elbow on the arm of her chair and aimed her straw at the ceiling. "You're probably right," she said. "But I need hard evidence, and I need to know you can get it without being blinded by your personal feelings." She sniffed and pinched her nose. "As for Joseph—at the moment, it's her word against nobody's when it comes to King's death. She may have confessed to you, but there's no record of it. Any half-decent defense attorney will have her deny all charges. The sole evidence against her is that video, but the victim only appears in a holohead and there's no footage of the actual death. It's all circumstantial. I wouldn't try it."

She leaned forward and rested her elbows on the island. "But if she says the Tongs were extorting her and we go after the Tongs, that's another story. Maybe we can't get them without getting her too. Or maybe she claims self-defense with King and plays up how the Tongs used her to hack Battle. A sympathetic jury might buy it. Not that there isn't some truth to that story, but it's a risk." She settled back in her chair. "So how do you want to play it?"

"I take it we don't have enough on the Tongs right now to make much of a case," I replied. "Like you said, it's her words and what I've scraped together on pure speculation. There's no hard evidence. Not of them extorting her. Not of them killing Giménez. I'm guessing you'll need that."

"We will," Yee said.

I looked at Moreno. "Anything you can do?"

"Officially?" He shook his head. "No. Not unless you want the Tongs to hear about it. If you tell me a citizen is in danger, no one wants that. If you can find evidence on the King and Giménez deaths, I can get it in the right hands. But if it all starts pointing back to the Tongs and the wrong people get wind of it ..."

"The Tongs will know." I looked at Yee. "So if we can get you that with Mirlande's help?"

"That might be enough." Yee twirled the straw between her fingers. "The Tongs are the bigger prize. Joseph would be facing a manslaughter charge for King, plus obstruction of justice for conspiring to move his body. But she could turn State's witness and claim self-defense. With no concrete evidence against her, we could drop the manslaughter charge. Maybe she'd get off with probation on obstruction if she gave us enough to make a case against the Tongs. Then we put Giménez's murder on the Tongs, along with fraud, theft and extortion for the hack."

"That sounds reasonable," I said.

"What about Battle?" Moreno asked. "Someone in her position won't enjoy hearing her name in connection with all this. If the Tongs can squash an investigation, so can Battle."

"She's a victim," I said. "The Tongs tried to rob her. If she plays it right, it could boost her image." I stamped the headline in the air above me. "'Rocket Mogul Shoots Down Organized Crime.' She could make herself a hero."

"It's something," Yee said. "More than I've seen on the Tongs in a decade, anyway." She palmed the straw and rested her hands on the arms of her chair. "But it needs help, and it won't be easy. We need direct evidence tying the Tongs to the Giménez murder. Plus, hard proof the Tongs hacked and defrauded Battle and iRise." She looked from Moreno to me. "Plus, we need names. Who made the deal with Joseph? Who initiated the hack? Who carried out the Giménez hit?"

She shook her head. "These guys aren't amateurs." She pointed her straw at Moreno. "Your friends will shut this down the second they hear of it. Enriquez and the rest of the Tongs know it. That gives them the liberty to do whatever it takes to keep this quiet. You know better than I do that you won't get much help and that this whole mess could get even uglier if Enriquez thinks he could go down for it."

She stabbed the straw at me. "As for you Carver, Moreno tells me you work civil cases, which in our state means combustion violations." When I didn't answer, she said, "He also told me you wouldn't divulge any details about your investigation or who you're working for."

"I don't mind telling you some of it," I said. "Yes, I'm often hired by clients looking to build a civil case. But they wouldn't hire me if word got out that I told anyone who asked who I was working for and why. As long as they're not hurting anyone else, everyone has a right to their private lives. We all crave that privacy." I nodded at her subterranean yard. "But I don't have to tell you that."

Yee laughed. It was the easy, confident laugh of a woman who sees the world in all its folly. "Mr. Carver, I had no idea. You play the hardboiled private detective, but deep down you're a starry-eyed idealist."

"Call it what you like," I said. "I worked my client's case as far as I could, but I stumbled into something bigger. Something that needs fixing. So here we are."

"Here we are." Yee's face grew stern. She leaned forward and folded her hands on the counter. "As for this case, I don't know you or your methods. Between the Tongs and Joseph, it seems like you're already in over your head. Moreno might like you, but it's the evidence and the law that matter, not his personal opinion or mine. I've known plenty of private detectives whose work doesn't hold up in court. So whatever you get me, it has to be something I can actually use."

SEVENTEEN

It was almost two in the morning by the time I left Yee's house. I needed to tell Battle about Mirlande and the Tongs. I needed to tell Schuyler I had finished the job he hired me to do and he could have some of his damn money back. But it was the middle of the night, and I was tired. Tired from an overnight stakeout in a rented car. Tired of billionaires playing their petty games. Tired of chasing pretty, stubborn women and fending off unwashed, self-righteous zealots and self-aggrandizing hackers and their hired muscle trying to work their way into every crevice of people's private affairs. Tired of the whole dirty system that pitted otherwise decent people against each other and gave the undecent ones an excuse to get even dirtier. So I sent Battle a brief message explaining how the Tongs had hacked her account and killed Giménez. Then I went home. Schuyler could wait until morning.

A weak yellow dawn was seeping through low gray clouds over the lake by the time my airtran touched down in Chicago. I made the walk home through the dusky streets as the earliest risers shuffled off to their commutes. I lived alone in a two-bedroom bungalow in Roseland, a kilometer and a half from the Pullman airtran depot. I'd bought the place as soon as I was drawing a steady paycheck as a cop. It wasn't a palace, but it was plenty big enough for me, it had a fully modernized kitchen and, at a time when most buyers were looking for subter homes like Yee's, the price had fit my budget. Having grown up in the neighborhood, I knew my neighbors and they knew me. Not well enough that we were having barbecues and watching football every weekend, but well enough that we could all live our own lives without people meddling in each other's business. I had paid off the mortgage a few years ago, when I still had a regular income, which meant I only had to scrape together enough of my current fits and starts of earnings to keep the lights and water on and pay the insatiable taxman.

I closed the front door behind me, poured myself a drink of the first liquor I could find, downed it in one gulp and fell into bed. I dreamed of Julia, her body splayed on the ground, blood running out from under her holohead as if from a leaky pipe fitting. She turned her head to look up at me.

"You're too late, Carver," she said.

I kneeled and turned off her holohead. A Tong skull stared back at me instead of what was left of her face. I switched off that holohead, only to see it replaced by Enriquez's dragon skull. His cold, cruel laughter rang in my ears. I remained kneeling, thumbing the holo unit again and again, even as the blood spilling down Julia's neck pooled on the ground around me. Enriquez's holo became Julia, became a Tong, became Julia, and her flesh and hair melted away until there was nothing but a human skull staring back at me. The blood rose over my shoes. I pulled the holo unit off Julia's collar and smashed it on the ground. The skull dissolved into Mirlande's face, her wide eyes staring up at me sightlessly, a single scarlet hole in the center of her forehead.

It was almost noon when I woke. I felt like I hadn't slept a minute. My head was clamped in a vise, and someone was stabbing a switchblade between my ribs. When I hauled myself to the bathroom and looked in the mirror, I saw bloodshot, heavy-lidded eyes and striped bruises the size and color of Japanese eggplants where the Tong thug had grabbed my left arm. I rubbed my eyes, which were drier than the New Dust Bowl. It felt like I was scrubbing my irises with sandpaper.

I staggered into the kitchen and brewed myself a mug of coffee. My stomach wasn't crazy about that idea. It wanted breakfast. My brain wanted a vacation. For once, the two were in alignment. In today's world, you could get pretty good food anywhere and fast. But great food still took time, and time was a luxury I was willing to afford on a day like that.

I had visited the Roseland Farm Co-op two days before I left for LA, so the fridge was fully stocked. I found butter, milk, eggs, fresh asparagus, some aged cheddar and the rest of a porchetta I had cooked last week. If I had possessed a gram of foresight before plunging into bed, I would have put some dough in the smart oven to chill, proof and bake while I slept. If I wanted to eat in the next hour, I didn't have time to bake anything from scratch. Fortunately, I had a few croissants I had cooked and frozen the previous week. I pulled one out and set it on the counter. Without time to thaw properly, the croissant would lose some of its flakiness, but I planned to hide it under the rest of my Benedict.

I turned the oven on and called Battle.

"I got your message," she said, "and Mirlande came to me this morning. So I think I know most of it."

I put a saucepan on the induction burner and set the screen control to low heat. I added an egg yolk to the pan and whisked it with a splash of lemon juice and mustard. "Did you check your accounts today?" I asked.

"I had my accountant in here first thing. No new withdrawals in the last fourteen hours."

"Good." I added a pat of butter and continued to whisk. "You talk to the police?"

"No," Battle said. "You said they couldn't be trusted."

"Not all of them, anyway." When the sauce was thick enough for me to see the pan between strokes, I took the pan off the burner, whisked in another pat of cold butter and a healthy portion of melted butter and added a dash of salt and pepper. "If you feel threatened or you think of anything that could help, call me or that cop I mentioned last night. Moreno. He's one of the good ones." I set the finished hollandaise aside and stuck the croissant into the oven. Then I put a pot of water with a splash of vinegar on the burner and set the control to boil.

"Are you still working this case?" she asked. "From what I understand, you don't handle murders anymore."

While the water heated, I cut off a slice of the porchetta and seared it in a pan with several asparagus spears. "Not officially," I said. "But I don't like being used, and I feel like some of Camila's blood is on my hands."

When the meat was slightly crispy and the asparagus was bright green and just tender enough to bite, I turned off the burner. My pot of water was simmering. I cracked two eggs and slid them gently into the bubbling water one at a time.

"Well, I don't like being used either." Battle's voice came out low and taut through my screen. "Not by my employees, and certainly not by criminals. I'm done sitting on my hands."

"What you do with Mirlande is up to you," I said. "She betrayed your trust, but I don't think she set out intending to hurt you. The way she tells it, she was trying to protect herself and you and got into a position where she couldn't back out. But the safest place for her right now is inside your house. As for the Tongs, I could use your help."

"What do you want me to do?"

While the eggs cooked, I took the croissant out of the oven, cut it in half and layered each piece with porchetta and asparagus. "You have money and influence," I said. "We'll need both. The Tongs operate with impunity because they have half the city in their pockets or by the balls. For things to change, someone needs to reset that power imbalance."

"I'll see what I can do. I'll get Chantal to help. She's tired of being cooped up here and she has influential clients." Battle ended the call.

When their whites were firm, I spooned a poached egg onto each croissant half and topped both sides with grated cheddar cheese. I popped the Benedicts into the oven to melt the cheese and brought the hollandaise back to a simmer before pouring it over the finished dish.

I had finished my coffee while cooking and brewed a second mug. I drank and ate slowly and thought about how I was going to get the goods on Enriquez and the Tongs. When I had finished breakfast, I called Schuyler. Cherrier put me through.

"You found something," Schuyler said.

"Yes and no," I said. "I found something. But it had nothing to do with combustion. Our agreement was eight thousand dollars for the first day, plus two thousand for every day after that. I'm refunding you two thousand dollars. When it comes to carbon pollution, Battle is as clean as one of your space stations' decon chambers."

"So what did you find?" Schuyler asked.

"I'm sure you'll hear about it soon enough."

"I'd like to hear about it now," he replied. "Where are you?"

"Home," I said. "Chicago."

"I'll tell you what. Fly out here and tell me in person. I'll pay you for your time and travel. After all, I hired you to investigate. I'd like to know it wasn't a complete waste of time and money."

I didn't have to think about it for very long. I didn't have any other cases lined up, and I wouldn't get much on the Tongs from three thousand kilometers away. "All right," I said. "Give me a couple hours." I started the dishwasher, made myself presentable and headed for the airtran depot.

On the corner of 105th and King, a girl and her mother had set up a folding table under a drooping elm tree and were selling lemonade. It was the kind of thing you didn't see anymore outside of places like Roseland.

As I approached, the girl said, "Lemonade, mister? Freshly squeezed. Only four dollars a cup."

I would have paid three times that if she'd spike mine with vodka, but I figured that wasn't an option.

The mother piped up when I looked in their direction. "We got scones and muffins too. Four dollars apiece."

I stopped. "How you making out?"

The girl beamed. "We got forty dollars already."

"Make a cup for this nice man, honey," the mother said. She leaned toward me as the girl scooped ice and stirred the pitcher. "You hear about the killing in Champlain Park?"

I hadn't.

"Sounds like two boys, too young and too stupid to be carrying guns. But they had them, or at least one of them did. Some words were said, and now one of those boys is dead." She pinched her lips together and shook her head. "That place has been in disrepair for years. Lights don't work. Grass is overgrown. Playground swings are just chains with nothing to sit on. Basketball hoops ain't got no rims. Reputable folks don't go there. So now it's the best place for doing things you don't want other people to see."

I knew the park, but I never went there. I guess that made me reputable.

"Anyway," she said, "we're raising money to clean the place up. New lights, some new equipment if we can afford it. I'll mow the grass myself if I have to. You know the city won't do nothing."

I thought if they continued at this rate, they would be able to afford a single streetlight bulb by the end of the day. But my mouth was dry from coffee and croissant, and it was a hot spring day that was only going to get hotter where I was headed. "Just the one cup," I said.

The girl's grin was so wide it was likely to split her face in half. I guess that's what it felt like to imagine you could solve the world's problems one glass of lemonade at a time. "Thanks, mister!"

I accepted the drink and continued my walk. The lemonade was better than I expected, cold and perfectly balanced between tart and sweet, like a hard truth delivered by a friend. But by the time I had finished the cup and reached the depot, the thought of going back to see Ellory Schuyler had turned the chilled refreshment to hot acid in my throat.

EIGHTEEN

I boarded the airtran and came face-to-face with myself. Only it wasn't me, and I wasn't looking in a mirror—the similarities ended below my double's chin. It was a woman wearing a holohead that somehow replicated the features of whoever was facing her. It was flawless. Outside of Schuyler's, the best I'd ever seen. The woman with my face stared back at me long enough to let me reflect on the incessant mimicry required to flourish in today's society—or something like that. Then she turned away, and her holohead transformed into the face of the man hunched over his screen on her right.

There was a slight jolt as the airtran began its vertical ascent. The seated passengers paid it no mind, and those standing bore it with a subtle tightening of their grips on the handrails. As it was late morning, the car was only about two-thirds full. A few passengers watched out the window as the ground receded below us. Most turned their attention to their screens, staring at the displays above their wrists only they could see.

The airtran leveled out and headed west, and for thirty minutes we cruised amiably through flawless blue skies above a bed of clouds. As we approached Denver and descended below the haze, I gazed north and west across the Rockies toward where the Lemhi Free State lay beyond the horizon. Then the land disappeared behind the peaks as we touched down, and I transferred to the LA-bound route.

The change was so imperceptible I didn't notice it as it was happening. We took off amid gray skies in Denver and emerged from the clouds somewhere around southern Utah. The skies were a crisp, pale blue as we soared over the Zion solar farms, but the LA skyscrapers hid behind plumes of black smoke, and the sky above the Pacific was an eerie red-orange. Aboard the airtran, the view tore passengers' gazes away from their screens one-by-one, so that by the time we began our descent, almost everyone was staring wide-eyed out the windows or glancing around the cabin at the unlikely group of strangers accompanying them on their plunge into the apocalypse. By the time we landed, it was as dark as twilight, though the sky still glowed like an unanswered distress beacon.

The doors slid open, and a stench like charred onion assaulted me, sharp, dead and sulfurous. No one was in a hurry to exit, and when I finally stepped outside, my diaphragm was working double-time to draw in the ash-thickened air. I blinked and squinted against the millions of invisible particles gusting into my eyes and moved quickly into the rental kiosk. I bought one of the last respirator masks off the rack, but they had sold out of protective eyewear. With one hand shielding my eyes against the grit-filled air, I found my rental—another Kwang—and directed it to Schuyler's.

The sky was the color of a tomato rotting on the vine all the way across town and up the mountain. The normally sparsely pedestrianed streets were now devoid of all foot traffic. The gleaming stucco buildings of Beverly Hills and Brentwood stood coiled, shuttered and tense, like soldiers awaiting a battle. The air was less noxious as I stepped out of the car in Schuyler's driveway, but the northeast wind whipping over the ridges assured me it would get worse soon enough.

Cherrier received me, looking as unremarkable as ever. I declined his offer of refreshment, and he led me down to Schuyler's office.

Schuyler waited behind his desk, wearing the same incongruous holohead. He was reclining comfortably in his chair with his hands folded across his stomach, but the office door had scarcely slid closed before he spoke.

"So," he said, "you found no evidence of a combustion violation."

"No," I said. "None at all."

"Pity." He shook his head. "But you found evidence of something else. Anything that might interest me?"

"Two deaths. One accidental, one intentional." I stood behind the chair facing his desk, looking down at him. "But you knew about the first one."

Schuyler's green eyes glittered malevolently. His usual half-smile stretched into a thin, hard line. "What are you suggesting?"

"Don't worry. I know you weren't responsible. Not directly, at least."

"So what are you accusing me of?"

I leaned forward, my hands resting on the top of the chair. "Naomi Battle didn't break the combustion law. But that's not why you hired me."

"It isn't?" He was trying to be disarming, but the bared white teeth behind his bloodless, semi-parted lips weren't cooperating. "I seem to recall telling you I had seen the smoke."

I considered calling him a liar to his face and decided against it. "You wanted to bring down Battle and thought you had an opportunity," I said. "Combustion was a convenient excuse. If you lived in Texas, you would have accused her of having an abortion. In DC, of firearms distribution. In South Dakota, of trans grooming. Anything the cops couldn't touch. You just needed an excuse to hire someone like me."

Schuyler waved away the suggestion with a careless flick of his wrist. "Tell me about these deaths."

I turned and walked to the window. Way out over the Pacific, the sky was still an innocent, unsullied blue. But the fire's corruption was spreading, and no matter where I looked, a jaundiced firmament seeped into my periphery. I glanced back at Schuyler. "You attended Battle's party to celebrate the Seashell contract on the evening of April fourth."

"So?" Schuyler had given up his attempt at charm. His digital face reflected the tension beneath it, the thin flesh drawn taut across the sharp bones below.

"During the party, you ventured out onto a balcony off the ballroom. You saw a man and a woman standing on an adjacent balcony."

Schuyler opened his mouth, but I cut him off. "Don't bother denying it. It's all on video." He closed his mouth and tried to find a neutral expression.

"The man went over the edge," I continued. "That left a Black woman in a gray dress, and you assumed it was Battle. It wasn't, but your actions had the same effect."

Schuyler bristled. "Are you calling me a racist?" He started to push himself out of his chair. "There's not a racist bone—"

"Sit down," I said. To some white people, there's no greater insult than reminding them they're still aware that their skin color is different from mine and that noticing this difference can lead to certain unconscious and unwarranted assumptions. "I'm calling you myopic. You saw what you wanted to see."

Schuyler paused halfway between sitting and standing, but then his mass seemed to get the better of him, and he slumped back into his chair, still glowering at me. "Perhaps you'd better get to the point, Mr. Carver."

"Gladly," I said. "You thought you saw Naomi Battle help a man to his death. You figured it would be a matter of time until she was arrested. After all, it happened at a crowded party. There must have been other witnesses. You waited for the police to do something, but they never did. Maybe you considered telling them what you saw. But if no other witnesses came forward and there was no physical evidence, you knew it would be your word against hers, and the police might think you were just gunning for your business rival. When the investigation died down, you sent Battle a threatening message. But she didn't know what the hell you were talking about, so the threat had no effect. That's when you hired me."

I squared my body to face Schuyler and took a step away from the window. "You knew if you told me what you had seen, I would have told you to take it to the police. So you made up a combustion charge to give me a reason to snoop around Battle's home. You figured there were two possible outcomes. One, maybe I'd discover something about Connell King's death. Something that would incriminate Battle. Or two, at the very least, my being there would spook her into doing something stupid. Well, you were right on both accounts. Almost right, anyway. Because, once again, Battle wasn't involved in King's death. Instead, my investigation set off a chain of events that led to a bunch of thugs with computers getting a little richer and an innocent woman winding up dead. More people may die before this is all over." I gazed once more at the glittering tiled roofs dotting the foothills below. "You're a rich man." I turned back to face him. "But I suppose a conscience is a luxury you can't afford."

Schuyler held my gaze, his jaw locked, and touched his screen.

"If you're thinking about calling the police," I said, "don't bother."

His hand dropped to his desk.

"They know. I told them everything I found. The DA knows. Battle knows. The only thing no one knows is that this whole mess started with you. An innocent woman is dead because you got jealous of a business rival and didn't trust the cops to do their job. If you call the police now, that's the only new information they'll learn."

Schuyler sat hunched over his desk, his forearms pressed against the unyielding surface, his face as cold and even as the stone of the furniture. His green eyes went from jade daggers to gleeful emeralds. His lips broke into his predatory half-grin. "I assume you have evidence of all this?"

I answered with a glowing smile of my own. "None whatsoever."

"Of course not." He rolled his heavy torso back in his chair. "So who did I see on that balcony? Who killed this Mr. King?"

"Like I said when I called this morning, I'm sure you'll hear about it soon enough."

"You're not going to tell me."

"No."

"I hired you to investigate—"

"And I did. That investigation is over. I'm a private detective, and you're no longer my client. It's not your privacy I care about."

Schuyler spread his fingers on the surface of his desk and pushed himself to his feet. "In that case, there's no reason for you to be here," he said. "You may go."

"I'll do that," I said. "In a minute. First, there's one thing I'm still not sure about. Battle said she thought of you as a mentor, that you were her friend. Was that ever true?"

He sneered. "You said it yourself, Mr. Carver. We're business rivals. Naomi Battle may be a fine lady, but in business, you either win or you die."

"Only you didn't win," I said, "and someone else died. I don't suppose that's good for business."

I turned and went before Schuyler could say anything else. Cherrier met me on the stairs and followed me to the front door.

As I exited Schuyler's mansion, another man had stepped out of his car and was striding toward the house. He was tall and slim, almost gaunt in an ascetic way, and his fine, lightweight suit hung loosely around his shoulders and hips. He had a prominent nose and dimpled chin in a well-heeled face that was now tanned, taut and weathered. His thin lips were pressed into a hard line, his blond hair was long and straight, but not unruly, and he had steely blue eyes that bored into your soul. I met his gaze and let him look into mine as we passed. The man's face made me think of the long-dead bald eagles still emblazoned on our national seal, his suit suggested a man of means, and his pious stare reminded me of Todd and River's. I waited for him to say something over his shoulder as he approached Schuyler's house. But evidently my soul was cleaner than I thought, because he entered the mansion without a word.

Schuyler's chauffeur parked the other man's car, came back, found me waiting and went to retrieve mine. I put on my respirator and stood there feeling about as good as was possible under an ashy yellow sky and a hot, noxious wind. I still didn't know what I was going to do about Mirlande and the Tongs, but I was glad to be rid of Schuyler.

The chauffeur swung my car around in a neat arc and stopped at my feet. I thanked him and got in. I was reaching for the gear knob when the unmistakable crack of a gunshot rang out from Schuyler's house.

NINETEEN

I lunged back out of the car and raced past the bewildered chauffeur to the front door of the mansion. But as I put my hand on the doorknob, I heard a thud that sounded like a slammed door at the back of the house. I darted around the humped entry level and reached the mountainside in time to see the blond-haired man picking his way down the treacherous slope below Schuyler's house as easily as a construction bot over steel girders. I considered chasing him long enough to realize the best I could hope for would be tripping him up as my unconscious body tumbled into him.

Instead, I returned to the front of the mansion and tried the door. It was locked. I pounded on it and shouted for Cherrier until he pulled it open. His stolid, bioplastic face had melted into drawn, stricken eyes, jowled cheeks and hanging jaw.

"Mr. Carver ..." He struggled to get the words out. "It's Mr. Schuyler. He's ... He's been—"

"Shot," I finished. I pushed past Cherrier into the house. "Show me."

Having someone to give him orders seemed to snap Cherrier back into his role. He led me through the sitting room and down the curved white staircase, far faster than I expected for a man of his age. Still, by the time we reached Schuyler's office, it was clear there was nothing to be done. Ellory Schuyler lay in a pool of his own blood with a pomegranate-red crater in his gut and a pistol at his feet. His

121

holohead's features had slackened against the dead face underneath, and the only twinkle in his emerald eyes came from the glimmer of the digital projection.

I kneeled at the edge of the spreading crimson stain and pressed two fingers to his carotid artery. But I felt nothing. He was gone. I stood and called Moreno to tell him what had happened.

"Jesus, Carver," he said. "You bring this much trouble everywhere you go?"

"Only if I can help it."

He sighed heavily. "All right. Stay there and don't do anything stupid. I'm sending someone over."

I disconnected and looked at Cherrier. His eyes had the dilated, red-rimmed appearance of someone who had just seen his first dead body, but his usual expressionless mask had settled back in place.

"You okay?" I asked.

"Yes, Mr. Carver," he said. "At least, given the circumstances, of course."

"Of course." I scanned the walls of Schuyler's office until I spotted a pinhole camera in the corner opposite the door. "Have a drink," I said. "It helps. For a little while, at least."

"Thank you, Mr. Carver. But I believe I've recovered myself." He steadied a trembling hand against his screen. "May I offer you something?"

"A coffee," I said. "If you can manage it." It was shaping up to be another long day, and Cherrier looked like he could benefit from having something else to do.

"Right away, sir." Cherrier tapped the order into his screen.

I inclined my chin toward the camera. "In the meantime, let's take a look at the security video."

Cherrier shook his head. "I don't have access to the footage of this office."

"But he does, right?" I pointed at Schuyler. At least he looked nothing like Julia. "I'm sure he'll let us look if we ask nicely."

Cherrier glanced down at Schuyler long enough to hold his screen to Schuyler's face, then averted his gaze. As I expected, we didn't need Schuyler's real eyes to pass the retscan. Cherrier pulled up the shot of Schuyler's office on his screen's display. I had him reverse the video until the blond man entered the room. He sat down in the chair across the desk from Schuyler. They spoke for about five minutes, and I could tell by the expression on Schuyler's face that he was enjoying their conversation less and less as it went on. Finally, he pulled a pistol from behind his desk and pointed it at the other man. The blond man stood and raised his hands to his shoulders, his palms facing Schuyler. Schuyler stepped around his desk and advanced on the other man, gun leveled, until they were about a meter apart. Schuyler said something. The blond man returned his words with a sanctimonious smile. Then he lunged at Schuyler.

He moved much faster than I, and evidently Schuyler, expected. Before Schuyler could react, the other man had seized his wrist and was wrestling for the gun. They struggled for a moment, their bodies twisting together, the weapon hidden between them, before Schuyler collapsed and the gun dropped to the floor.

The blond man backed away, the shock written across his face replaced quickly by the self-righteous certainty I had seen as he passed me on his way into the house. He turned, strode to the door and exited.

Cherrier closed the video and clasped his hands behind his back. "Your coffee is ready, Mr. Carver."

I followed him back upstairs and waited while he retrieved my coffee. It was as good as I remembered—dark, bitter, pitiless.

"Do you know that man on the video?" I asked.

"His name is Gabriel Eindhoven," Cherrier said.

"What did he want with Schuyler?"

Cherrier raised his chin and stared at my forehead. "He said they had business to discuss. Mr. Eindhoven was a ... friend of the family."

"I can tell," I said. "Did you happen to hear what they were discussing?"

I thought I saw Cherrier's lips twitch, which I supposed was the closest he got to betraying offense. "No," he said.

"He come by often?" I asked. "This family friend?"

"No, Mr. Carver, not often. But I came to know Mr. Eindhoven fairly well over the years."

"Any idea why he and Schuyler might want to kill each other?"

"No."

I sipped my coffee. We were standing in the mansion's entryway, facing the white-walled sitting room. From that angle, I couldn't see the mountainside or houses below, but way out beyond the full-length window, the metronomic cobalt sea rushed up to meet the descending void of the pale blue-gray sky in an unbroken line flatter than a dead heartbeat.

"Let's try this," I said. "When was Eindhoven last here?"

"About a month ago." Cherrier checked his screen. "Yes. March tenth."

"Was he here to discuss some private business with Mr. Schuyler on that occasion as well?"

"I believe so. He had an appointment. But I don't know what they discussed."

"Did Eindhoven have an appointment today?"

"No." Cherrier faced me with his shoulders drawn back and his features locked in place. "I wasn't expecting him. But Mr. Schuyler agreed to see him anyway."

"And you have no ideas about the nature of their business together?"

He gave a slight shake of his head. "No, Mr. Carver."

Detective Maggie Conway showed up thirty minutes after my call to Moreno. She was a short, squat woman a few years shy of retirement who refused the stairlift and creaked her way down to Schuyler's office, leaning on the railing and placing two feet on each step before descending to the next one.

As we crept down, I told her what I had seen on the security footage.

She continued her painstaking descent with no visible reaction. "I'll look at the body first."

It was a good thing Schuyler was dead, because a less patient man would have given up and left by the time we reached the crime scene. Conway paused in the doorway to catch her breath and survey the room. Then she circled the office in a series of tightening spirals.

I stood at the doorway and watched her work. "Moreno sent you?"

Her eyes scanned the room as she continued her circle, favoring her left leg. "He did."

That was good enough for me. Eventually, her spirals closed on Schuyler's body, and she came to a stop at his feet. She scanned his body, circled him once more and stopped at his side. Placing both hands on her thigh for support, she lowered the other knee to the ground and bent over him.

"Lead deposits around the wound," she said. "Looks like a contact shot."

I stepped up next to her and noticed the faint charcoal smudges on the less bloody patches of Schuyler's shirt. Some detective I was. I had missed them in my haste to see if Schuyler could be saved.

"The fabric around the bullet hole is singed too." She reached down to Schuyler's collarbone and switched off his holohead.

The real face underneath the holo matched his body, but he wasn't Ellory Schuyler. This man's face was round and soft, with gaping, watery brown eyes and thinning, lank, sandy hair. He looked to be in his mid-thirties, maybe early forties, but far younger than the sixty-eight-year-old Schuyler.

Conway looked at me. I looked at Cherrier.

"Who's this?" she asked.

"That is Mr. William Schuyler," Cherrier said. "Ellory Schuyler's son."

"Tell her about the man who shot him," I said. "This Mr. Eindho-ven."

Conway started. "Gabriel Eindhoven?"

"That's correct, Detective," Cherrier said. "He was William's school friend."

I turned to Conway, my head spinning.

"I don't know about this school," she said, "but right now, he's the leader of California Right to a Future."

TWENTY

Conway had held the CSIs back until she was done with the scene, but their arrival made the office more than a little cramped, so Conway, Cherrier and I made the slow climb back up to the top floor sitting room. The space was dimmer than I remembered, the skylight above me obscured by a leaden haze. We arranged ourselves in the unarranged, marbly furniture.

"You'd better start at the beginning," Conway told Cherrier. "What happened to Ellory Schuyler?"

Cherrier glanced at me.

"The public won't hear it from me," I said. "Some of it will have to get out sooner or later, but I'm sure the Schuyler estate and the LAPD can reach some agreement on the details."

Conway gave a curt nod of assent.

Cherrier's shoulders and spine relaxed from steel rods to aluminum. "It was just over a year ago," he said. "April first. Mr. Schuyler—Ellory—did not wake at his usual hour. At eight o'clock, I went to his bedroom, thinking he might be ill and in need of my assistance. His room was empty, his bed undisturbed. I searched the rest of the house, but Mr. Schuyler was nowhere to be found. I tried to contact him through every channel I knew of, but he did not respond.

"Aside from his unexpected absence, I had no reason to be concerned. He was in good physical health, his business was thriving, and I had served him long enough that I had no reason to suspect he was engaged in any dealings of a nefarious sort. He was still grieving the loss of Mrs. Schuyler, but all things considered, he seemed to be bearing the weight of her passing rather well. He may have been bereft, but not to the extent I ever believed he would harm himself.

"So I waited a day. When Mr. Schuyler still did not return, I called William. He took the situation in hand at once. The most important thing, we decided, was to safeguard his father's legacy until he could be located. If the public learned about Ellory Schuyler's absence, everything he had worked for—his company, his innovations, his ambitions—would have crumbled to bits. William would assume control of his father's company immediately. He was living in Boston at the time, but he arrived the evening of the day I notified him."

"And no one but you and William knew about Ellory's disappearance and William's ascension?" I asked.

"No, sir," Cherrier said. "Not to my knowledge."

"What about Eindhoven?" I asked. "Did he know he was meeting with William and not his father?"

"I couldn't say," he answered. "As you saw on the video, William wore his father's holohead in Mr. Eindhoven's presence. But I don't know what was said behind closed doors."

Conway cut in before Cherrier could continue. "You said there was security footage of what happened between William and Eindhoven. Was there any footage that might shed some light on Ellory's disappearance?"

"None that I'm aware of, Detective," Cherrier said. "I know none of the cameras captured Mr. Schuyler leaving the house on April first or the previous night."

"But all the footage was there?" Conway asked. "Nothing was destroyed or altered?"

"Not that I'm aware of," Cherrier said. "But I'm not a detective."

Conway pressed on. "You said there was no exterior footage of Schuyler leaving the house. What about the cameras inside the house? Did they pick up anything?"

I thought that if I had half of Conway's investigative instincts at her age, I would count myself lucky.

"There were no cameras inside the house at that time, Detective," Cherrier said. "William had them installed after he arrived."

"Was Mr. Schuyler in the house on the evening of March thirty-first?"

"Yes."

I studied the video of the Martian landscape on the wall over Cherrier's left shoulder. The swirling wind was still throwing rust-colored dust against the desolate, smoldering sky. For all I knew, Ellory Schuyler could have run away to Mars, leaving the rest of us to deal with the mess on Earth. I wouldn't have blamed him.

"When did you last see him that night?" Conway asked.

"Around ten o'clock. I brought him a drink and asked if there was anything else he needed. He said no, that I was welcome to retire for the night."

Conway made a note on her screen. "So William showed up on April second. What happened then?"

"I kept Mr. Schuyler's disappearance from the rest of his domestic staff," Cherrier said. "The day William arrived, he had me offer them extremely generous severance packages and glowing letters of recommendation. They had previously signed non-disclosure agreements as a condition of their employment, and I had no reason to believe they suspected Mr. Schuyler was anywhere besides a business trip. I was confident only William and I knew of his disappearance."

"So William fired the rest of his staff and kept you on," Conway said. "Sounds like you took on some extra responsibilities."

"Yes, Detective," Cherrier replied. "Temporarily. Only until William hired replacements."

"Did you receive a raise for your exemplary service?"

"No." Cherrier's features did not move, but his voice came out tighter than carbon fiber. "And I didn't expect one."

Conway held his gaze for a moment, then returned her attention to her screen. "Tell me again why you never notified the police about Ellory Schuyler's disappearance."

Cherrier drew himself up in his chair. "I serve Mr. Schuyler's interests. I do so with discretion and by anticipating his needs and desires." He inclined his head toward Conway. "What would the police have done if I had reported his absence?"

Conway glanced from her screen back to Cherrier. "We would have looked for him. And if something happened to him, we would have had a much better chance of learning the truth a day after he disappeared than we do a year later."

A shadow stole over the room as a cloud or gust of smoke passed overhead. Out the window, the ocean continued its tireless, rolling march against the unrelenting sky.

"Yes," Cherrier said. "You would have looked for him. And inevitably, the story would have gotten out that Ellory Schuyler was absent. There are many capable people at Schuyler Space Industries. But none of them is Ellory Schuyler."

Conway was unaffected by the assault on her own powers of discretion. "You said you serve Ellory Schuyler. Present tense. Are you in contact with him now?"

"No, Detective."

"Do you believe he's still alive?"

"I don't know."

"If he was alive, can you think of where he might have gone?"

Cherrier's face remained impassive. "I serve Mr. Schuyler's interests, Detective," he repeated. "If Mr. Schuyler is alive and well, I must assume he does not want to be found."

Conway matched his poker face. "All right, Mr. Cherrier. I'm going to check on my CSIs. Then I'd like to see that security footage you mentioned."

I peeled myself out of the form-fitting chair and tagged along as Cherrier led Conway on the plodding trek back downstairs. I waited at the opposite end of the hallway while he escorted her back into

Schuyler's office.

He came back down the hall and acknowledged me with a slight bow of his head. "Mr. Carver, I'm sorry to have involved you in all this."

"Not your fault," I said. "I'm almost certain you didn't murder Mr. Schuyler."

Cherrier's expression twitched in the direction of a grimace. "Of course not. Still, I have to thank you for the decisiveness and tact with which you handled the situation."

"That's the job," I said. "You have your role, and I have mine."

I started up the stairs. Cherrier followed and overtook me without ever seeming to hurry.

"Can I offer you anything else before you go?" he asked.

"No, thank you." We climbed a few more steps before I said, "You told Detective Conway no one at Schuyler Industries had the same qualities as Mr. Schuyler." I kept my voice quiet, hoping to keep Cherrier from retreating further into his role as the stoic gatekeeper. "How did the company fare under William?" I had a feeling I already knew the answer.

Cherrier stopped and turned back to me. He curled his lips inward. "I couldn't say for certain."

"You must have seen things, heard things." I gestured in the direction of Schuyler's office. "William's dead. You can't hurt him now. But you might be able to shed light on why he was killed."

"I sensed an unevenness," Cherrier said. "A lack of direction, perhaps."

I glanced at my screen as Cherrier spoke, sorting through a summary of Schuyler Industries' stock prices and quarterly forecasts.

"William meant well," Cherrier continued. "He was very well-educated, of course. And intelligent, perhaps even more so than his father in some ways. But he lacked Ellory's passion for the company and its work. I'm not sure anyone else in the company put a finger on it, but from the conversations I heard, I sensed they noticed something was missing."

"William was twenty-five years younger than his father. And he was at least twenty-five kilos heavier, wasn't he?"

"Yes, Mr. Carver."

My screen vibrated against my wrist, but I ignored it. "Didn't anyone notice the change?"

Cherrier gave a stiff shake of his head. "William didn't appear in public. He used a voice modulator and wore his father's holohead constantly. If anyone saw him on video, it was from the neck up."

"But he went to Naomi Battle's party."

"That was his first public appearance in a year. He didn't want to go, but everyone around him told him he had to show his face to keep up appearances. His father would have gone. I knew that, and so did William."

We reached the top of the stairs.

"Will you be needing anything else, Mr. Carver?" Cherrier asked.

My screen vibrated again. There was a message from Battle: "Mirlande is gone."

TWENTY-ONE

I left William Schuyler in the capable hands of Conway and Cherrier and directed the Kwang down Schuyler's ridge and up Battle's as fast as it would go. Twin clouds of dust thrown up from below and ash raining down from above obscured my view of the road, as well as the valley and coastline below. The LA scenery wasn't exactly living up to the holodisplay hype. I called Moreno and told him about Mirlande first.

"Any idea where she might have gone?" he asked.

"No." The Kwang plunged deeper into a dirty gray haze that might have been fog or smoke. "She mentioned a friend in the area, but I never got a name. My best guess is she didn't want to bring anything else down on Battle and decided to run instead."

"Battle have any ideas?"

"I'm not sure. I'm headed there now."

"All right," Moreno said. "I'll put out an APB and check the cameras around Battle's."

"Thanks," I said. "I'll update you once I learn more." Then I filled him in on Schuyler and Eindhoven.

"This just keeps getting better and better." He sighed. "Well, if my guys are looking for one person in the area, they can look for two. I'll add Eindhoven to the list. Any idea why he'd want to pop Schuyler? Or vice versa? And did Eindhoven know which Schuyler he was dealing with?"

"I don't know about the second question," I said, "but I have an idea about the first. The greenies I met snooping around Battle's were Eindhoven's crew. When I showed up, they complained to Eindhoven, and he went to Schuyler to tell him to back off."

Outside, the wind howled through the mountain passes and buffeted the car. Black shrouds had settled into the valleys. The few plants I could see through the haze clung desperately to the mountainside. Eddies of debris whipped against the car's windows as it rounded corners where the wind swirled in the pockets of the mountain.

"So this all comes back to you," Moreno said. "Aren't you modest?"

I laughed. "When you make enough enemies, you learn to know when you're not liked. The three I met outside Battle's weren't happy to see me there."

"But Eindhoven wouldn't have known you were working for Schuyler unless—"

"Unless Schuyler hired Eindhoven's crew in the first place," I finished. "Schuyler wouldn't have told Eindhoven about me. But if he hired the greenies first, Eindhoven would have known Schuyler was searching for a combustion case against Battle. When I showed up, Eindhoven thought Schuyler had soured on their agreement."

"As a reason for Schuyler to pull a gun on him, it seems a little thin," Moreno said.

I agreed. "We're missing something."

"Maybe he knew it was William under that holo and threatened to expose him unless William called you off."

The Kwang began to climb, and the smog gradually sloughed away until I could make out the slope of the mountain on one side and the precipitous cliff's edge on the other. "But according to Cherrier, William didn't want anyone else to know he was playing dress-up."

"So Eindhoven figured it out on his own. They were friends.

Maybe William said or did something his father wouldn't have."

"Maybe," I said. "It's the best we have so far, anyway. If you collar Eindhoven, he might tell you."

The Kwang swung out to the north side of a ridge, and the sky blazed red and orange above the shadowed upthrust shards of the city skyline. Then it curved around a bend, and everything two meters above the road disappeared in the soot-filled haze. As bad as the fires were, Schuyler and Battle's mansions would be safe. There was half a city between them and the infernos, and aside from Schuyler's oaks, which might double as a natural firebreak, there was hardly anything up there to burn. I wondered if the two multibillionaires had singed away the remaining vegetation after they bought their land for that very reason.

"But why did Schuyler hire the Futurists in the first place?" Moreno asked. "If you're half the investigator you make yourself out to be, Battle's clean. Why would Schuyler knowingly waste money chasing hot air?"

I took Moreno's words as a compliment and told him so.

"I'll be impressed when you have actual evidence against the Tongs," he said.

For the moment, I was stuck on Schuyler. "Business went south when William took over. He didn't have his father's touch, and he couldn't figure out how to turn things around. Meanwhile, iRise was taking off. William was getting desperate. Schuyler's butler told me William and Eindhoven were old friends. So I bet William turned to Eindhoven for help. He told Eindhoven he suspected combustion, but he was really looking for a way to harass Battle."

"It sounds plausible," he said. "Petty, but plausible. And it's the same reason he hired you."

"He admitted as much."

"Not exactly thinking outside the box."

"No," I agreed. "But that wasn't William Schuyler's strong suit. He wanted someone who could get inside Battle's home, and he'd already been investigating her under false pretenses. Hiring me was an easy next step."

"At least this part is relatively straightforward," Moreno said. "I'm still waiting for Conway's report, but it looks like we have all the evidence we need against Eindhoven. Now we just have to find him. What else do you need on the Battle-Joseph front?"

The Kwang swept onto Battle's ridge—or at least I thought it did. I couldn't see much through the clouds of dust and smoke. But I felt the car ascending, and soon the smog parted enough to give me a glimpse of the Pacific.

"I'm almost there," I said. "Let me find out what Battle knows and get back to you. In the meantime, do you know the name Ostin Torres?"

"No. Should I?"

"He was Mirlande's in with the Tongs. A cousin of her friend. If the Tongs get to Mirlande first, he might be useful."

"I'll add him to your list and see what we have on him," Moreno said. "If we can find him, I'll have someone bring him in."

The Kwang neared the place where I had first spotted Eindhoven's greenies, one creeping along above me and the other on the opposite ridge. The mid-afternoon sun cut through the haze enough for me to catch the shadow of the adjacent mountain, looming like a dormant beast.

"So you think the Tongs took her?" Moreno asked.

"I think they'd like to." The Kwang slowed as it neared the triangular gate blocking the road, but the barrier swung open before the car came to a full stop. "And things aren't looking great at the moment."

I ended the call. I didn't like where any of this was heading. There were too many interests involved, and they were all out for blood. I knew what came of desperate people pushed to the brink.

As the Stone King-Aazadi-citizen turf war had escalated during my first days in Homicide, the Event Horizon quickly deteriorated into an urban siege. Residents retreated to their homes. Stone soldiers patrolled the otherwise deserted streets, but their bosses stayed out of sight. And every day, there were more fresh bodies. Any detective who caught a homicide in those weeks faced the same uphill battle. No surveillance, no evidence, no witnesses. The few people we could find who would say anything gave us the same answers: they weren't Stones, they didn't know any Stones, they weren't even sure the Stones existed. Between the two warring gangs, everyone in and around the Event Horizon had become terrified of being mistaken for a Stone or a snitch, either of which meant a death sentence.

Every homicide detective in the city was working overtime as the body count continued to climb. We caught a few breaks and solved some of the killings. But not enough. The Stones and the civilians living under them were at the brink of an all-out war. The brass ordered increased patrols of the Event Horizon. But there weren't enough beat cops on the force to be everywhere at once. The city instituted an eight p.m. curfew for most of the South Side. The Stones and their vigilante adversaries broke it. People were murdered in broad daylight.

Finally, the brass sent in tactical units with orders to treat everyone in the Event Horizon as a potential threat. The detectives were out of time. The city was going to put an end to the violence, even if it meant a lot more people had to die in the process. To everyone in the Event Horizon, those units were an invading army. The Stones and the civilians under them may have been at war, but they all liked cops about as much as an aural mold infection. And they trusted us even less. I was pulled from my cases and reassigned to tactical intelligence. I continued my investigations between my official shifts. I still believed the sole way to minimize the bloodshed was to bring the individual killers to justice and uncover the Aazadi—assuming they existed.

The Kwang continued up the road to Battle's place. A gust of wind kicked up a cloud of bone-dry dust and spattered the car with ash. The gate hadn't even closed behind the car when something punched a pair of holes through the front and back windshields.

TWENTY-TWO

I heard the glass rupture and saw the new ventilation holes someone had installed in the Kwang's windshields. Then somebody else took a plasma cutter to my right shoulder. I ducked down between the wheel and the seat and reached a hand up to my shoulder. It came away red and sticky. I slid it under my shirt and felt the furrow the bullet had carved in the flesh above my clavicle. It was more than a graze wound, but I would survive. The poor visibility and the Kwang's autodrive probably saved my life. On a clearer day, the sniper's bullet that had come through the rear window would have likely shattered my skull instead of slicing harmlessly through the front. And if my hands had been guiding us through those snaking cliffside roads when someone started shooting at me, there was no telling where the car might have ended up.

Instead, the Kwang continued up the road with nothing but a warning message on the dash screen. I kept my head down, tore off my unbloodied left shirt sleeve and wrapped it around the gushing wound. Whether the road had curved behind a shield of rock or the sniper considered their job done, there was no second shot. The Kwang passed inside the electrified fence. A minute later, Battle's mansion materialized out of the haze above me, its faux stucco exterior looking even paler against the charred sky.

Battle was waiting for me in her driveway, wearing goggles and a respirator. She ran toward me as I stepped out of the car with a crimson stain spreading down my chest. "What the hell happened?"

"I think the Tongs finally kept their word," I said.

Battle put an arm around my waist and practically dragged me inside.

"Good thing too," I continued. "They were starting to disappoint me."

Battle pulled off her face coverings. A fine layer of soot outlined circles around her eyes and mouth. "What are you talking about?" She guided me toward the elevator.

"Better not." I inclined my head at the pink and black mosaic beneath my feet. "I'd hate to bleed all over your fancy tiled floor."

Battle didn't even waste time rolling her eyes. "Come on." She punched the elevator call button and pushed me inside when the doors opened. "We have a first aid kit upstairs."

We rode the elevator to the second floor through a cloud of ash. The medical bag Battle pulled out of a cabinet in the iRise conference room was as much of a kit as Battle's top floor suite was a room. It looked like she had brought home a military trauma pack as a souvenir from her time in the Air Force. She covered a corner of the conference table with a tarp and ordered me to sit. She removed my makeshift bandage and cut away my bloody right sleeve. I watched as Battle flushed the groove the bullet had carved into my shoulder with an antiseptic solution.

"No major damage," she said, "but it's pretty deep. We can get away with a couple of microstaple patches for now, but if it opens up again, you'll need a more secure closure."

Working with practiced efficiency, she dried the skin around the injury, pinched the tissue together and applied three patches and a gauze bandage. When she was done, she stepped back and looked me over. "You okay?"

I shrugged my right shoulder. It had felt better, but everything seemed to be working well enough. "Yeah. Thanks." I tapped my screen. "Looks like I'll need some new clothes."

"When you're done with that, you'd better tell me about the Tongs keeping their word."

I placed my order and told Battle about Enriquez's threat and the apparent sniper. "My best guess is they were waiting on the ridge next to yours."

"You think they're still there?" she asked.

"Probably not," I said. "Even if they know I'm still alive, I doubt they're waiting around for the cops or someone else to find them."

Battle's lips curled into a scowl. "Camila was bad enough." She blew out a slow exhale through her nose. "I'm going to make these assholes pay."

The drone arrived with my new clothes. Battle had them sent up and gave me the room to change. I wrapped my bloody rags in the tarp and deposited the bundle in the square, silver robot waiting with Battle in the hallway.

"Tell me about Mirlande," I said.

"Her car is still here." Battle tilted her head in the direction of the garage. "We have video of her leaving on foot. Come on. I'll take you to Dev."

I swore under my breath. Mirlande was proving to be more hard-headed than I had suspected. "Did you speak to her after we talked this morning?" I asked.

"No." Battle rubbed a smear of ash from her cheek. "I haven't seen her since she confessed her role in all this."

We stopped outside Chaudhri's office.

"Maybe I should have stayed closer to her after we spoke." Battle sighed and shook her head. I couldn't tell if she was frustrated with Mirlande or herself. Probably both. "I knew she was upset, but she seemed to have herself under control." She pushed her tongue against her upper lip. "And after what she did, I couldn't stand to look at her."

"You had every right to be mad at her," I said. "I don't like the way she handled things either. But if you want to blame yourself for

Mirlande taking off, don't waste your energy. Mirlande was going to take things into her own hands, no matter what. I'm guessing she didn't want to be responsible for another Camila. You could have followed her all night and all morning, and she would have still come up with an excuse to step away for a minute."

"You're right." Battle faced me with her eyes knife-sharp and her jaw set. "I'll deal with her when this is all over. But I won't let her get hurt trying to make up for what she did."

"I'll find her," I said, though the odds of doing so in time were dwindling by the minute.

"Good." Battle knocked on the office door and pushed it open.

Chaudhri stood leaning into his computer displays but turned toward us as we entered.

"Show him," Battle said.

He pointed at the security footage on one display. Mirlande exited the front door of Battle's mansion and turned east, toward her car and the garage. Chaudhri had spliced footage together, and as Mirlande was about to leave the range of the first camera, another one picked her up. She walked around the east side of the house, passed her car and slipped along the side of the garage. Another camera followed her briefly as she made her way down the side of the mountain behind the garage. Then she disappeared in the haze and the folds of rock.

"Is there a trail there?" I asked.

"No," Battle said.

"Any other cameras looking down the slope?"

"No," Chaudhri answered. "But at one fifty-seven p.m., she turned off the security dome. It was off for about a minute, then she switched it back on."

I walked to Chaudhri's west-facing window. Through the darkening haze, I could just make out the shadowed chasm where Connell King had met his end. I doubted Mirlande had chosen that path. She didn't seem the type. But that didn't get me much closer to where she had gone.

I glanced back at Battle. "Have you tried calling her?"

"Yes," Battle said. "Several times. I think she turned her screen off."

"Did you talk to your staff yet? Maybe Mirlande confided in one of them."

"No. I haven't had the chance yet."

I surveyed the footage on Chaudhri's displays one more time. "I'd like to do that. Domestic and professional."

"All right," she said. "I'll have them assemble downstairs."

"No," I said. "One at a time. If Mirlande talked to one of them, that person is less likely to reveal it in front of everyone else."

I waited in the ground floor sitting room, well aware that Battle's employees had gone through the same thing when the police found King's body the previous morning and ten days before that when he first went missing. It wasn't a pleasant time to be employed by Naomi Battle. They cycled through, one after the other, and I asked each of them when they last saw Mirlande, what they had said to each other, how Mirlande was behaving. I didn't expect much, and I got even less. No one had exchanged more than a few words with Mirlande in the last twelve hours. No one had seen her leave or knew where she might have gone.

When her last employee had returned to work, Battle rejoined me in the sitting room. "Now what?" she asked.

I stood and walked to the door. "Keep trying to reach Mirlande. If you hear anything, let me know."

"What are you going to do?"

"Go after Mirlande. Make sure she isn't lying on the side of the mountain with a broken leg."

TWENTY-THREE

Battle followed me to the front door. I donned my respirator, and she offered me her goggles. I put them on and plunged back out into the noxious air. I circled to the side of the house, following the path I had seen Mirlande take on the security video. The wind at my back drove me forward and blew dust and ash past my legs and over my shoulders. I stood between Battle's mansion and garage and stared down the slope to the secluded, pristine houses nestled in the foothills and out to the Pacific below. It was steep, but not the sheer drop King had experienced on the west side of the house. It looked like the right direction for an escape. Then I examined the dust at my feet.

As a former city cop, I had little experience tracking people through the wilderness. But I found the partial footprints behind the garage easily enough. Just over the rim of the mountain, I saw a bush with a broken branch that seemed like a natural handhold. I stood at the edge and surveyed the terrain below me. It looked challenging enough, and I told myself a city boy like me could use a strenuous hike in the refreshing mountain air. It was too bad about the air. The slope descended at roughly a forty-five-degree angle, steeper in some places. About twenty meters down, the chain-link fence wrapped around the mountainside. Shelves of rock offered foot- and handholds for someone with feet and hands as slim as Mirlande's. They didn't look like they'd help me as much. The descent was broken sporadically by patches of flat earth, not wide enough to form a trail, but wide enough for the dust to settle and hopefully record footprints. The slope was dotted with the same sparse vegetation as the rest of the mountain: yucca and chaparral bent but not broken by the wind sweeping over the ridge. But mostly, it was five hundred meters of rock and dust spilling down to the sea. I focused on searching for signs of Mirlande's trail and started to descend.

When I reached the fence, I saw prints on either side, but no gate in the barrier. I called Chaudhri and had him switch off the dome, then scaled the three-meter-tall barricade and lowered myself carefully to the steep rock face on the other side. I continued down with a grudging admiration for Mirlande's stubborn resourcefulness. After a few steps, I was left without vegetation or a rock shelf for a handle. I eased my way down the treacherous slope, leaning back, my toes squeezing through my shoes for purchase on the angled slab. I glanced up once to see a ledge some ten meters below, then returned my attention to my feet, counting down my steps from thirty as I went. Before long, I was sweating under the late afternoon sun that had crept around the haze. My shoulder ached, my breath came hard and fast through the respirator, and my goggles were fogging up. When the terrain finally leveled out, I tiptoed onto the edge of the narrow shelf, tore off the goggles and scanned the dirt until I found a partial toe print. I had no way of knowing if it was Mirlande's, but as hard as the wind was gusting up over the mountains, I didn't figure prints would last long in this earth. Whoever had passed this way had done so recently.

I looked down over the slope and found the next shelf and what seemed the easiest route to reach it. Then I stepped over the edge and continued my descent in firm, choppy steps. When I had taken another thirty paces, I lifted my gaze and saw the next ledge was still another twenty meters down. As I did so, my foot slipped in a film of dust or ash coating the smooth stone. I crashed down onto my right hip, and then I was sliding, picking up speed as I skidded down the mountainside. My hands groped for any seam. My toes scrabbled for footholds. I scanned the rapidly passing rock for a bush, a weed, a stem—anything to help me break my fall. But there was nothing within reach.

My feet hit the shelf with a jolt, and for a moment, my momentum seemed great enough to take me head over heels over the edge, tumbling down the next precipitous rock face. But I flexed my knees to cushion my landing and threw my weight forward against the slope. I pressed my body and face to the stone like a baby at its mother's breast and wormed my fingertips into whatever crevices I could find.

When I felt stable enough to move, I slid one hand to my face and removed the respirator. The air still smelled like charred onions, but there was a bracing undercurrent of salt coming up from the sea, and I felt better with the wind on my face than I did sucking air through a filter tied over my nose and mouth. I stayed there a minute, trying to catch my breath and let my heart rate come down. I succeeded with the first of the two. I looked down but didn't notice any footprints on the ledge that weren't mine. Either I had erased them during my graceful landing or Mirlande had found a less exciting path. Turning my head to glance over the edge, I saw a winding stretch of pavement another two hundred meters down the slope. Above me, I could make out the upper level of Battle's mansion over the mountainside. I told myself I had descended far enough that I was as likely to die by trying to climb back up as I was continuing downward. Either way, it would end with me falling and breaking my neck, so there was no reason to delay that outcome by going back up.

I crouched, eased my feet over the edge and resumed my descent. The incline wasn't completely vertical, but it was steep enough that I had to use my hands as well. I continued like that for at least ten minutes before the slope leveled out a bit and I was able to stand and walk. I could see the road below clearly now, close enough that I knew I could make it, but far enough that I wasn't ready to take stupid chances. I crept down the slope for another fifteen minutes, my eyes scanning the surface for loose stones or dirt that might provoke another slip. When I needed to search for the easiest path, I stopped. I tried to work my way from bush to rock to flat ground, anything that might break my next fall. But I made it to the road below with no further mishap.

In the dirt beside the road, I found a clear, small footprint that I took for Mirlande's. All around it was a series of jumbled partial prints. A smudge of dirt edged onto the narrow carbocrete shoulder. It looked like someone had taken several choppy steps in roughly the same spot and skidded—or was dragged—out toward the street. I didn't like it.

I walked left and right along the road, looking for more prints. I found none. I crossed the street and called Moreno.

"I was about to call you," he said. "We caught Eindhoven shortly after we last spoke. The holier-than-thou prick didn't even have a holo unit on him. A beat cop saw him walking along Sunset Boulevard, carefree as you please, and took him in. From what Conway told me, it didn't take long for him to confess either. Apparently, he sounded almost eager to go to trial. He'll claim self-defense and tell the world about Schuyler's so-called corruption."

"Corruption?" I said. "I'm no saint, but that seems a little harsh for my role in all this."

Moreno gave a short, dry laugh. "You had it mostly right. Eindhoven wasn't too happy about Schuyler choosing you over his guys. But it seems young William was also using Russian carbon-fired steel for his rocket parts."

"So Eindhoven threatens to go public about Schuyler's illegal steel, and Schuyler pulls his piece."

"That's about it," Moreno said.

I discovered a new depth of disgust for William Schuyler. All this time wasted on a nonexistent combustion case, and he was the one using dirty steel. But someone had to clean up his mess, and I had been dumb enough to volunteer. I told Moreno about the Tong sniper.

"You're one lucky bastard," he said. "The only person who has benefited from these fires. I'll check out the other ridge, but like you said, whoever shot at you probably cleared out."

I told him about Mirlande wandering off and how I'd followed what appeared to be her trail. "Looks like it ends here." I sent him my coordinates. "Did you check the nearest cameras?"

"Yeah," he said. "Nothing."

I scanned the dirt on the side of the road opposite the mountain. Nothing there either. "I think she's been taken."

I sent Battle my location, and Chaudhri picked me up and drove me back to the mansion. We made it without incident. Either the Tong sniper had cleared out or they were only looking for my rented Kwang. I told Battle what I had seen on the road below and what I believed it meant.

"The Tongs." Battle's nostrils flared.

"That's my first guess."

"What do we do now?" she asked.

The short answer was that we would have to wait. Wait and hope Moreno could find Torres or pick up something on one of the city's surveillance cameras.

We didn't have to wait long, but the call came to Battle's screen, and it wasn't Moreno. When the voice on the other end spoke, Battle's eyes jumped to mine.

She put the call on speaker. "What?" she said. "Who is this?"

"We have your girl," a synthetic baritone voice said.

"Who?" Battle said. "Mirlande? Mirlande Joseph?"

"Yes. You have twenty-four hours."

"How do I know you have her?" she asked.

An image appeared on her screen, and she swiped it up into a holodisplay. It was Mirlande, her eyes wide and hair frazzled, but her delicate jaw set in a firm line and her chin raised to the camera in defiance.

"You have twenty-four hours," the voice repeated. "You will receive an account number. Send twenty million dollars by five p.m. tomorrow, or she dies. And we will make sure the entire world knows you let her die."

TWENTY-FOUR

The call ended.

"I won't pay them." Battle paced away from me, her fists clenched at her sides, then pivoted and marched back. "I pay them once, and they'll come back the next week and take somebody else. It won't stop."

She might have been right. From everything I knew about the Tongs and the cyberpunks like them, once they wormed their way into a system, they bled the host dry. Of course, things looked a lot different when stopping the bleeding meant letting someone else die.

"All right," I said. "Let me fill Moreno in." I sent him a message.

"Sit tight," he replied. "The only lead we have right now is Torres. One of my beat cops told me she has eyes on him. But I want to bring him in without the Tongs knowing."

"More waiting," Battle said when I looked up.

I nodded.

"Well, we don't have to do it here. Come on."

She led Chaudhri and me to the elevator and up to the third-floor library. I ordered a tequila from the bot in the corner in honor of Camila. Battle let the mechanical barkeep touch its metal finger to her tongue, and it mixed her a glass of something colorless, cloudy and slightly viscous. Chaudhri sensibly opted for water with lemon.

Battle apparently noticed me eyeing her drink. "Would you like one?" she asked. "You'll have to give a microneedle blood sample the

150

first time, but it's worth it. Each drink is tailored to your body chemistry and your current nutritional, hormonal and situational demands. You'll never want coffee again."

"I'll pass, thanks." I sank into a plush mycoleather armchair. I was all for individuality, but I preferred my libations to be hammers rather than scalpels.

Chaudhri settled into a chair on my left and busied himself with his screen, his right leg vibrating with restless energy. Battle circled to the western window and stood there, sipping her stimulant cocktail and staring out across the undulating, shadowed ridges. The low evening sun outlined her figure in blood and fire.

"I would have helped her," she said, her back to me. "If she had come to me first, I would have helped her."

I downed a swig of tequila. "You don't have to convince me." I stared at the amber liquid and thought of Camila sipping her own drink at the end of her day and of her lying face down in the dirt. I thought of Mirlande, lost, alone and less than twenty-four hours from death. And I thought of Julia, long since dead in the middle of a Chicago street.

The simmering tensions between the cops, the Stones, the Aazadi and their civilian proxies had all boiled over one sweltering August night. Whether the Stones pulled facial recognition data from the cameras just outside the Event Horizon or they used the feeds they had hacked in their own territory, I still don't know. But shortly after midnight, the tactical units in the area found themselves under attack from Stones dressed in Chicago PD uniforms and wearing holoheads identical to the cops who had patrolled the area.

I had been chasing a lead at an address on the eastern edge of the Event Horizon when the shooting started. As the tactical units pressed forward block by block and the Stones fought back, I was caught in the crossfire. Fighting my way out wasn't an option. Even if I could tell cop from Stone in the dim pearly glow of the streetlights, both sides were primed to shoot anyone with a gun. Three times I waited until the battle moved past me. Each time there was a break in the shooting, I picked my way east until the next battle closed in.

Julia's unit was ambushed near Aberdeen Street. By the time I got close enough to see who was who, it was all but over. Julia and her killer were dead. The other cops took care of the remaining Stones. It took me several minutes to convince the few who survived that I was one of them. Not that I could have saved Julia anyway. She was gone before her body hit the ground.

When the sun finally ascended above the blood-stained streets, there were no more battles left to fight. But everyone knew things couldn't go on the way they had. The civilians couldn't stomach any more bloodshed, cops were unwilling to fight a war in their hometown, and the ongoing conflict was costing the Stones soldiers and money. After three days of wound-licking, a trio of corpses was discovered hanging from the Kedzie Avenue Bridge. Digital intelligence traced their identities to some low-level hacks committed earlier that year. The Stones had exterminated their rivals.

The Aazadi had the right idea. Lacking the numbers and resources to challenge the Stones directly, they had waited for a moment of internal crisis and stoked the fires of public anger. But they were too few and too impatient. They had pushed things too far and couldn't protect themselves when the Stones turned their attention to the real problem. The government of California didn't have that issue. And in a state of forty-five million people, the government only needed a small percentage of zealous proxies eager to fight their neighbors on its behalf. Far fewer were willing to stand up to thugs like the Tongs.

Meanwhile, Battle was taking her own trip down memory lane. She was still facing the window, and her voice started out as barely more than a whisper. "I've known Mirlande for almost ten years. We met when she was in college and I was working for NASA. One of her professors assisted with the final assembly and testing of spacecraft. He often brought Mirlande and one or two other students with him." She turned away from the window and sank into an armchair across the room from me. "At the time, I was the backup astronaut for the lunar phase of the Castor-Pollux II mission—parallel manned voyages to the moon and Mars. I trained with the Castor crew in case one of them was unable to take part in the mission. I was working on the simulator as the engineers were running their tests. We wanted to make sure all the controls handled the way they were supposed to, in case the automation went down. I noticed a little more drag on the lander than I had in the JSC simulator. Mirlande was acting as the liaison between the astronauts and engineers, so I mentioned it to her."

She stared down at her glass. "Anyone else would have let it go. Mirlande's professor, the other engineers, even flight ops—everybody deferred to the astronauts. They would tell you if you were doing something stupid, something that would jeopardize you, a crew member or the mission. But everyone knew the astronauts were the ones who had to deal with the equipment a million kilometers into space. As long as everything worked, the next most important thing was that the astronauts were comfortable. So anyone else would have made a slight adjustment if it was within tolerance, or they would have smiled, nodded and ignored me if it wasn't possible. But not Mirlande. I forget her exact words, but she explained in the nicest possible way why my discomfort was a good thing, why the system was designed the way it was and how it would help me in space."

She looked up at me and downed her drink. "I knew right then I wanted her to work for me. I brought her on as an intern when I started iRise two years later. When she graduated, I hired her full-time."

I studied the bookshelf stocked with actual books I doubted anyone ever read, the place where my combustion investigation had tipped Mirlande to the fact that I wasn't who I said I was. It was a nice story. It was the kind of story people tell about an estranged family member who was dead or dying, the kind of story that puts both the speaker and subject in the best light, despite everything that came between them before the end. It was sweeter than the latest zero-calorie sugar substitute, and the aftertaste was just as bad.

"Where did Mirlande sleep last night?" I asked.

Battle stared at me exactly the way you'd stare at someone who'd ignored the most heartfelt story you'd ever told. "Here." Her lips pinched together. "In one of the fourth-floor guest rooms."

"Did anyone search her room today?" I glanced from Battle to Chaudhri.

Battle shook her head.

"No," Chaudhri said. He looked at Battle. She gave a tight nod. "Should I be looking for anything in particular?" he asked me.

"No," I said. "If there's something important, I'm sure you'll see it."

I waited until I figured he had made it down the hall and onto the elevator. Then I said to Battle, "Why didn't you fire Connell King?"

Battle stared at me for a long time, her arms crossed. Finally she said, "Because he was good at his job."

I sipped my drink. The tequila was rich, oaky and smooth on my tongue. It tasted worth every dollar Battle had paid for it. "His job was to protect you and the people close to you." It was true, and it was a hard way to say it. But I was in that kind of mood.

She gave me a look that said no one ever talked to her that way, and I waved goodbye to my chances of taking Mirlande's tactful chief of staff job. But I had to hand it to Battle. She took her time, but she didn't hide and she didn't back down. She stood and walked to the bar. The bot poured her something that didn't look like a vitamin cocktail. She took a long drink and turned to face me, the glass in one hand and the other resting on the bar. "What have you heard?"

I relayed what Camila had told me. I mentioned Jordan Thompson, Battle's former trainer.

"It's true," she said. "In general, at least." She threw back another slug of her drink. "I never witnessed any of it firsthand. And he was at least smart enough to never come on to me. Or I wasn't his type." She gave a bitter smirk. "But Jordan came to me, and I heard stories from other employees. But there was no hard evidence. Just their word against his. I warned Connell. I put measures in place to isolate him while he was at work. But it wasn't enough."

She paused, as if expecting another question. But I didn't feel like asking one. I gazed down at my empty glass. None of it mattered now. Thompson was gone, King and Camila were dead, and time was running out for Mirlande.

"I know," Battle said. "If I had taken care of Connell, none of this would have happened. Then, if Mirlande ever found herself in trouble, she would have trusted me enough to let me help her."

"And if I hadn't shown up, or if I had figured out what was happening sooner, none of this would have happened either," I said. I had antagonized Battle enough. She hadn't killed anyone. And if we were going to get Mirlande back, I would need her help.

I was helping myself to another drink when Chaudhri returned. As expected, he reported that the room looked like it had never been occupied.

We waited almost two hours before Moreno called me back. "We got Torres."

"Did he give you anything?" I asked.

"He said he doesn't know for certain the Tongs have taken Mirlande. If they did, he claimed he wasn't a part of it. But he said when the Tongs have ransomed victims in the past, they've used one of three locations: desert areas near Agua Dulce and Chino and an abandoned rail yard in Carson. They're all outside LAPD jurisdiction and they all give the Tongs plenty of space to see anyone coming or going for kilometers in all directions. The Tongs throw up a holodisplay that blends in with the landscape. If anyone ventures close enough, it looks like there's nothing to see."

"Does that work?" I asked. "A display that big?" I had once seen a holodisplay large enough to disguise an entire room. But even the advertising displays stretching over the highways got a little translucent at the edges farthest from the projectors.

"I've never seen one," Moreno said. "Not that I know of, anyway. But I wouldn't put it past these guys."

I looked at Chaudhri.

"It's conceivable," he said. "Technically, they're not holograms, since they don't use recorded interference—"

"And non-technically?" I said.

He shrugged. "You ever see a twentieth-century hologram? They're laughable compared to today's three-D projections. And today's projections keep getting bigger and clearer. It's possible the Tongs are ahead of the curve or know someone who is."

"Anyway," Moreno said, "once the Tongs get paid, they take off, leaving the hostage behind. After they're clear, they disable the holodisplay."

"So what's the next step?" Battle asked. "You send flyers over those three sites and drop a SWAT team on Mirlande's location?"

Moreno didn't answer.

"What?" she said. "Am I missing something?"

"Just so we're clear," Moreno said, "you're unwilling to pay the ransom. Is that right, Ms. Battle?"

"That's right."

I saw where this was headed and knew none of us were going to like it.

Moreno sighed. "Then I'm afraid there's not much I can do."

"Not much you can do!?" Battle shoved her chair back and jumped to her feet. "You're the police. Isn't that—"

"Ms. Battle—"

"No. What good are the police, if even the supposedly honest ones—"

I stepped in front of Battle. "Just listen."

Battle looked from me to her screen and back again. Her shoulders relaxed ever so slightly. "Fine. Tell me."

"Carver was a cop," Moreno said. "So he understands. But I'll spell it out so we're all clear. Let's say this was happening in LAPD territory—which, according to Torres, it isn't. I guarantee there are cops in the department who know what the Tongs are up to. Any mobilization of enough LAPD officers for this thing to work would get the attention of at least one cop in the Tongs' pockets. Plus, it's not happening in LA. LAPD can't just swoop into Chino or any of these towns without alerting the local authorities first. Besides, I don't know anyone in these three departments well enough to trust they aren't on the take."

"So you won't help us," Battle said.

"I didn't say that," Moreno replied. "Hypothetically speaking, if I or another police officer from any department had concrete evidence that a crime was being committed or had been committed, we could take action. And, hypothetically, if I knew that a person or persons were threatening, pursuing or attacking innocent civilians, I would have to intervene."

I could tell Battle wasn't going to listen to Moreno much longer. "I think I should continue this discussion with Ms. Battle alone," I said.

"Yes," Moreno said. "I think you should."

Battle ended the call, her eyes blazing at me. I hoped her glare was meant for Moreno.

"I won't pay them," she said. "I don't care what he said—"

"Moreno can't help," I said. "If he tried the way you want him to, it would only make things worse. But that doesn't mean ..."

Battle raised her chin, and the fire in her eyes went from an inferno to a pair of blowtorches. "That doesn't mean I can't do something."

"Right. Moreno couldn't tell you that. And he couldn't hear you say it."

Battle stepped forward, her eyes locked on mine. If the two Tong heavies who had beaten me up had been in that room, she would have tried to strangle them. I wouldn't have bet against her.

"I won't pay them," she said, "but I will pay you. You bring Mirlande back alive, and I'll pay you a million dollars."

That was more than twice what I made in a year as a cop. I wanted to save Mirlande too, but a suicide mission wouldn't help anyone. "We'd need a plan," I said. "I can't just walk into a hostage situation against a dozen Tongs."

"We'll think of one," Battle said. "I'll help you. We'll get Mirlande back. And once this is all over, I'm going to bury those assholes."

TWENTY-FIVE

Money could buy a lot of things. An M meant I wouldn't need to take on a new case for a long time. Or at least I wouldn't need one to pay my bills. And I was confident Naomi Battle could use her impressive wealth to make life very difficult for the Tongs. But aside from paying the ransom, money alone wouldn't save Mirlande.

That wasn't stopping Battle though. "So we need to find them first," she said. "We can take a flyer over each of those three sites. We use IR to see through the holodisplay. When we find Mirlande, we go in and get her."

I shook my head. "We're not a SWAT team. If the three of us go in there, guns blazing against who knows how many Tongs and a hostage, we're more likely to spook the Tongs or shoot Mirlande than rescue her."

"Do you have a better idea?"

I had lots of better ideas. Ideas that wouldn't get me killed. Ideas that would have kept me out of this whole mess in the first place. But I hadn't acted on any of those good ideas so far, and I figured I might as well be consistent. I said, "I go in alone. Assuming there aren't too many Tongs, I'll have a better chance of keeping the situation under control. If things go south, you can take your revenge from the flyer."

"You'll need a holo."

I pulled up my screen display and ran a search. "A white skull. Simple. Día de los Muertos-type. Shouldn't be hard to find."

Sure enough, an array of samples appeared on my display.

"Will that work?" Chaudhri asked. "Surely an undercover cop would have tried that by now."

"Let's find out." I sent Moreno my search results and asked if any of them looked like Tong holoheads.

He responded almost immediately. "Most of them do. But it's not that easy. Every Tong holohead is embedded with a one-D code. They're pretty basic, but the Tongs change them constantly. They know if any holo doesn't have the right code."

I recalled the vertical lines I had seen on the foreheads of Enriquez and his goons. "I'm guessing you can't get the codes," I said.

"Not for long," he replied. "Seems like as soon as we get eyes on one, they change it. No one I know has ever replicated it successfully."

That almost bricked me. I needed to get close for this plan to work. I was as much of a sniper as I was a Green Rice farmer. And even if I deleted one Tong from distance, any others would do the same to Mirlande before I could get off a second shot. Then I remembered the woman on the airtran with the mirroring holohead.

I described it to Chaudhri. "You ever seen one of those?"

"No," he said. "Must be new. And from the way you described it, expensive."

"Will it work?"

He shrugged. "In theory, sure. At least if you're dealing with one Tong. But you said this woman's holo changed when she looked from you to another passenger. So if there's more than one Tong—which there surely will be—and they have different holoheads—"

"Mine will change when I look from one to the other," I finished. That could pose a problem. I had a habit of looking where I wasn't supposed to. "If there are more than two of them, it's a suicide mission anyway," I said. "It wouldn't matter what my holo looked like. But if it works, it should get me close enough for one Tong to see the code and believe I'm one of them. I just have to hope that leaves me enough time to act before my holo changes."

"We'll scope it out beforehand," Battle said. "If there are more than two Tongs, we'll think of something else."

I didn't love it, but it was the best plan we'd come up with. I ran another search and found what I was looking for. Like Chaudhri said, it was brand new, proprietary and very expensive.

I looked at Chaudhri. Chaudhri looked at me.

"How much?" Battle asked.

"Ten K," I said.

"Let me see."

I sent the listing to her screen. She took a few minutes to scrutinize her display. Then she tapped her screen. Mine lit up with ten thousand dollars in my account.

"If it doesn't work, I won't have to pay you a million dollars," Battle said before I could speak. "If it does, well, it will be worth it."

Spoken like a true businesswoman, I thought. I thanked Battle for her concern for my well-being, paid for the holohead and uploaded the file to my unit.

"Let's test it out," I said. "I want to know what to expect before I go in there."

We found some space in front of the western windows. The sun had gone down, and all that remained were the twinkling lights of the houses below and the vast, darkened expanse of the Pacific. I had Battle stand forty-five degrees to my left and Chaudhri forty-five degrees to my right. I pressed my holohead unit to my collarbone and turned it on, looking straight ahead.

"Nothing," Battle said. "It's still your face."

That wasn't promising. My face was about to get me killed. I reached up to the unit. Turning to Battle, I said, "Is it—"

"There it is," she said. "You look like me."

"Look closely," I said. "Is it your face, or the mirror image of your face? If this thing shows the mirror image of the Tong's code, I'm dead."

Battle aimed her screen at her face and glanced back and forth between her camera and my holohead. "It's not the mirror image. As far as I can tell, you look the way other people see me."

"Dev, what do you see?"

Chaudhri studied us from my right. "Don't look at me." He circled behind me and examined us from my left. "Your profiles are different when I look at them from the same side." He circled back to my right. "But your left and right profiles look the same. I think it's working the way you need it to."

"I need it to fool gangsters holding a woman hostage and eager to kill me," I said. "Is it working?"

Chaudhri walked around me once more. "Yes."

My screen lit up. Los Angeles County was ordering the evacuation of seven neighborhoods near the fires.

Battle glanced at her screen. "That's not us. We're fine."

"All right." I turned my holo unit off. "Let's try that again." I looked straight ahead and turned it back on.

"Still me," Battle said.

I turned and looked at Chaudhri.

"Now it's me," he said.

I turned and looked at Battle.

"Now me," she said.

I turned the unit off again, looked straight ahead and turned it back on.

"Still me," Battle said.

I looked at her. "Dev, tell me when it switches." I turned my head slowly from Battle to Chaudhri.

I was almost looking straight at him when he said, "Now."

"So it comes on as the last person I was looking at," I said, "except for the very first time, and it doesn't change until I'm practically staring at a new person."

"Then you need to be staring at a Tong before you turn the unit on," Battle said. "How's that going to happen?"

"We get one of the skull holoheads I found earlier. It doesn't have to be perfect. We just have to make sure the code would be right by the time a real Tong gets a close look at it." I pointed my thumb over my shoulder. "Can we use your ballroom?"

The last time I had been there, I hadn't known what had taken place in that ballroom. This time, the massive space felt even colder and emptier. I walked out to the nearest balcony and stepped up to the railing to see if my descent down the mountain had lessened my aversion to heights. It hadn't. I returned to the ballroom on less than steady legs, ignoring Battle and Chaudhri's quizzical expressions.

"Go stand at the far end," I told Chaudhri. I turned on the holohead and looked at Battle.

"It's me," she said.

"Tell me when it changes," I yelled over my shoulder. I turned and walked slowly toward Chaudhri.

When I was about fifty meters away, he said, "Now."

I stopped. "Could you read a code on my face from there?"

"Not clearly," he said.

I switched off the unit and sighed. "It's workable." That was the best I could say for our scheme. "I stare at the dummy Tong holohead before I go in and I turn the unit off so it doesn't get confused. I enter the holodisplay far enough from the Tongs that they don't suspect what I'm up to and can't read the code on my forehead. As I approach, I stare at one of them to make sure I pick up his code."

"Sounds like a plan," Battle said. I appreciated her confidence in my expendability. "We ready?"

"Almost," I said. "I can't just stroll into the Tongs' holodisplay. Even if I look like them, they'll see me coming a long way off. I need to get in close enough that I can act quickly, without them noticing my approach."

"You mean some sort of distraction?" Battle asked.

I nodded. "One that will get their attention but won't spook them into doing anything reckless."

"You have something in mind?"

"Maybe." I called Moreno.

TWENTY-SIX

Boldin met us in the entryway to see us off. She'd already convinced two of her clients, a screen star and a singer, to demand the city do something about the Tongs. I didn't know how far that would go, but it was a start. She embraced Battle, then Battle and Chaudhri took one of her flyers and headed for the Carson rail yard. A mechanical bot in Battle's garage patched the Kwang's windshields, and I retraced the route I had taken when I tailed Mirlande to her meeting with Torres. The night sky had an unnatural purple tinge and, as I rode the highway east, the glow of the downtown skyscrapers to my left was muted and diffuse behind a film of ash. In East LA, I exited and waited at the junction of four freeways, close enough to arrive in Carson or Chino within the hour if Battle and Chaudhri discovered the Tongs at either site. To the south, Battle scoped out the land below as she flew, looking for the most suitable spots for a Tong holodisplay. Chaudhri wore infrared lenses with a video feed linked to my screen, and together we searched for heat signatures Battle couldn't see.

The rail yard consisted of two plots of land—one trapezoidal, the other triangular—divided by a state highway. At about three square kilometers, it was the smallest of the three potential sites. For whatever reason, the old tracks had never been converted to run maglev trains, and the vacant land was never redeveloped. There was a homeless encampment in the northeast corner, where people took shelter in a dozen abandoned cargo containers. On my screen, burnt orange rectangles stood out against a backdrop of flat, featureless, deep purple that extended south and west to what looked like a dried-out channel. On the other side of the channel was an array of circular, bright yellow towers that I took for a biofuel refinery. Battle descended for a closer look. We all counted seven people gathered around the cargo containers, but since Battle could see them too, they weren't hiding behind a holodisplay. Aside from that, the site was just more empty land reclaimed by the desert. Battle pulled up and headed east to the second location.

"Any bets?" Chaudhri asked. "On where the Tongs are hiding?"

My screen's display showed an endless field of violet studded with blocks of amber and topaz and split by bands of onyx—the stunning and eerie monotony of the California landscape in IR.

"Chino," Battle said. "Get ready."

"Carver?" Chaudhri said.

"Agua Dulce." The last location on our list meant less time to rescue Mirlande and a longer, more challenging escape route. I was ever the optimist.

"Stakes?" Chaudhri asked.

"Steaks," Battle said. "A steak dinner for the four of us when this is all over."

Cut amber buildings yielded to unpolished amethyst land as the flyer neared its destination. As its name suggested, Chino Hills State Park comprised about thirty square kilometers of rolling, dusty hills. There was still some land that technically belonged to the California State Park system, but no one seemed to give a damn about it anymore. The trails were invisible from above, there were no signs, and the few remaining buildings were slowly succumbing to nature. Most of the land around the perimeter of the park had been bought up and redeveloped. In daylight, I figured the surrounded wilderness looked like a brush fire waiting to happen, an undulating sea of dried brown grass dotted with a few islands of greenery.

Any one of those hills would have been an ideal spot for the Tongs to hold a captive under the cloak of a holodisplay. No one could have approached the summit without the Tongs seeing them from at least as far as the adjacent hill. Battle took her time crisscrossing the land below while Chaudhri and I scanned the area in IR. But in the end, we found nothing.

"Carver wins." Chaudhri looked at Battle.

She returned his gaze, her face a grim fluorescent yellow on my screen. "We better hope so."

"I'll take my steak medium-rare," I said, "on the side of a double pour of Scotch." But my victory felt hollower than an empty stomach. I directed the Kwang toward Agua Dulce.

Battle flew north, crossing over the mountains a safe distance from the fires and the plumes of dense black smoke. I headed northwest, through the dense steel and glass forest of self-contained mini-city skyscrapers. The buildings erupted beside, over and around the freeway, their glittering lights flashing past me like shattered dreams. Beyond that urban bulwark, I passed between the dried-out river and even drier hillsides into a desolate corridor of biochar and mycelium factories. Near San Fernando, the opposing traffic thickened against a swelling backdrop of fire and smoke. The Kwang continued toward the mountains north of the city, skirting west of the oncoming blaze. The southbound lanes of the freeway were now packed with cars streaming away from the fire zone and into the protective enclave of LA. The wind drove the haze after them, sending black clouds down to the road. Between the night and the smoke, I could see nothing but the faded headlights of oncoming cars, the overarching holo advertisements—flickering in the gloom as the sensors struggled to pick up license plates—and the fires creeping down the mountainside.

Battle and Chaudhri reached the site long before I did. Unlike Chino and Topanga, Vasquez Rocks was on the federal historic register, which kept it out of the grubby hands of California legislators searching for a quick cash infusion. As the Kwang edged closer to the inferno, I distracted myself by scanning Chaudhri's live IR feed of the four-square-kilometer area below. From what I could see, their visibility was far better than mine.

"The wind is blowing away from us," Battle explained. "It's pushing the smoke toward the LA side of the mountains. I can see the fires well enough. But it doesn't look like they're headed this way."

Through Chaudhri's lenses, I saw a stark, arid landscape reminiscent of the Martian scenes displayed in Schuyler and Battle's homes. There was scarcely any vegetation, and the earth was studded with jagged rock formations, enormous slabs of boulder pushing up at odd angles as though an earthquake had torn up the land only a week ago, leaving behind splintered, upheaved plates.

Meanwhile, the Kwang sped forward in utter darkness. The dense smoke now obscured the city lights behind, the fires ahead, the night sky above. On my screen, there was more blackness: the smooth, empty earth torn by the charcoal and dusky purple shadows of the rocks. Battle reached the end of the park and banked the flyer back for another pass. As she turned, a flash of yellow pierced the night.

"I've got something," Chaudhri said. "Do you see that?"

The feed flickered with a faint wave of illumination as Battle cast the flyer's headlights toward the apparent heat signature.

"No," she said.

The yellow pixels centered on my screen, shrank momentarily as Battle ascended and expanded again as she flew closer.

"Still nothing," she said.

The splash of light brightened from golden through cream to pure white and resolved into three separate figures.

"Is it them?" Battle asked.

"Could be," Chaudhri said.

"Stay on that heading," I told her, "and don't go any lower."

Ahead of me, the smoke was filtering away. Red taillights peeped through the haze. Rocky slopes materialized on either side of the road. On my screen, the three figures grew larger and brighter.

"It's them," I said.

Two were standing. The third sat on the ground. I knew it was Mirlande even before Chaudhri zoomed in close enough to get a look at her face.

"Yeah," he said. "Two Tongs."

One more than I had hoped for, but not impossible—if I could surprise them.

"Keep flying," I said. "Don't change course until they're no longer visible."

"All right," Chaudhri said. "We'll meet you here." An address appeared on my screen.

TWENTY-SEVEN

In reality, Julia Noi never wore a holohead. I only caught the end of the ambush as I was trying to get back to my car while the Event Horizon came apart around me. What do you do when you come face-to-face and muzzle-to-muzzle with yourself? Julia hesitated. By the time she got her gun back up, it was too late. The Stone wearing her face let off a sputtering salvo from his machine pistol. Julia's muzzle flashed once, twice, in the gray pre-dawn, but she was already going down. Forensics later tied at least one of the bullets that struck her killer back to her gun. The surrounding cops finished off the Stone. By the time I finally got to her side, her face was an unrecognizable mess of gore. The surviving cops in her unit were restraining injured Stones and tending to their own wounded while the city burned all around us.

As the Kwang drove closer to the LA fires than I had been thus far, the blaze loomed over my right shoulder and lit up the road like the dawn. But it was pursuing other prey, lunging down the mountain-side toward the sparkling, sprawling city at my back. The smoke streamed away behind me as I caught up to the traffic fleeing north, and the freeway funneled us all forward into the untarnished darkness. I passed the guttering lights of Santa Clarita and headed north-east, following the northern edge of the mountains into the desert and a clear night sky.

After fifteen minutes, I turned off the highway and onto a road that snaked along a dried-out riverbed. Battle and Chaudhri were waiting outside Battle's flyer when I pulled into an overgrown clearing surrounded by the splintered remains of wood-frame structures that looked to be part of a long-abandoned campground. Battle donned the skull holohead she had purchased, and I put on my mirroring one. Chaudhri stood behind me while I stared at Battle long enough for my holohead to match hers. Then I turned mine off and hoped it would remember.

Within a few minutes, our distractions began to arrive. Moreno had called every confidential informant he knew and told them there would be a bottle of their choice waiting for them as long as they drank it at a specific location. Pretty soon, we were surrounded by over twenty vehicles. The three of us passed out the drinks the CIs had requested. Battle sent the designated coordinates to each vehicle's nav, and the CIs mounted up.

"Ready?" she asked me.

I checked the pistol—a 40 caliber Glock with electronic ignition—in my shoulder holster one last time. "As I'll ever be."

"We'll be watching you," she said. "As soon as you're clear, we'll be there to pick you up."

I got in shotgun with one of the CIs, and our caravan pulled out. We swept through the darkness, down an otherwise empty two-lane road. In the mountains behind us, the fires glowed in a dirty orange sky. But ahead of us, the night was quiet and still.

"What's all this about?" my driver asked. She let the car navigate the route we had given her, but she sat with both arms extended, hands gripping the steering wheel, fingers drumming slowly on its surface. In the faint backlight from the blazes and the ebb and flow of streetlights, her baby-faced holohead was sluggish and ghostly, its big blue eyes heavy-lidded and lifeless.

"It's better you don't know," I said. "Enjoy your night and go on your way in the morning."

She glanced at me, saw me watching her and turned away. We

wound between mountains on both sides, then turned north. The slopes receded behind us, and the desert took over. Then the rock formations burst out of the earth, shadowy and menacing in the darkness. The road led to a parking lot, and we kept going, through the empty carbocrete rectangle and out onto a desert trail. The ground was dry and hard-packed, and we drove smoothly through the wisps of dust kicked up by the vehicles ahead of us.

We approached the Tong holodisplay from the west, where there was a gap between the rock formations wide enough to allow our group of cars to pass. Moreno's CIs swung past where the Tongs were hidden and continued east, hopefully close enough to get the Tongs' attention without provoking them to do anything drastic. Our car was last. I got out before it came around the rocks and strode toward the holodisplay.

I couldn't tell if the projection blended seamlessly with the surroundings. In the dark, it worked just fine. Even knowing what to expect didn't prepare me for going from an empty desert to a hostage situation in the blink of an eye. As the last CI's car sped away in the distance, the two Tong thugs materialized before me, illuminated by a solar lantern whose light formed a halo around them. Between them, Mirlande was seated on the ground, her hands bound behind her back.

The Tongs stood facing away from me, watching our diversion recede in the distance. I stared down the one closest to me, knowing the entire plan depended on my holohead unit picking up his face as soon as possible. He turned, looked at me and froze. He was about my height but twenty kilos heavier and built like a walking, talking version of the boulders surrounding us. With my head fixed on him, I darted my eyes toward his partner, who was taller and only slightly less broad. They looked like the two heavies who had introduced me to Enriquez outside the diner.

When the shorter one spoke, his cavernous voice confirmed my suspicion. "Where'd you come from?"

"Back there." I cocked my head behind me without taking my eyes off him. "What's with the traffic?"

The gaping black eyes in his holohead narrowed. "You tell me."

"How should I know?" I said. "I was sent to check on things. I saw those cars, left mine out of sight and followed them on foot. Did they get inside the holo?"

"No."

"You sure?"

"Who the fuck are you?" the tall bruiser yelled in his nasal voice.

I was close enough to see the codes on both of their foreheads, which meant they could see mine—assuming the holo was working right. "You don't recognize me?"

"Boss never said anything about more guys," the shorter one said.

The taller one reached behind him toward his waistband.

I kept walking. "I guess he doesn't trust you as much as you think."

The tall man drew a pistol and held it loosely with the muzzle pointed down. "Who are you?" he shouted again.

I continued to move forward, angling my steps to put the shorter Tong between me and his pistol-wielding partner. "You first," I shouted back. I closed to within a few steps of the Tong nearest to me.

"Stop him!" the taller one shouted.

Over the shorter thug's shoulder, I saw the other man's gun hand begin to rise. I reached for the pistol in my shoulder holster. The shorter Tong's hand went to his waistband. The tall man got his gun up, but I was quicker. I put a bullet through the barcode in his holo-head before he could pull the trigger.

The shorter man drew his weapon, but I lunged forward and got my free hand on his wrist as he brought the gun around. It didn't stop him, but it slowed him enough for me to step inside the path of his arm. He reached toward me with his free hand, but I wasn't about to let him get his waste compactor grip around me again.

I whipped my pistol up in a short arc and slammed it into his temple. The crack of steel against his skull was more satisfying than a gunshot. He gave me the same fiendish grin as the last time I'd hit him. His hand circled my arm and stopped. His black eyes widened. Then, his hand fell away, and he went down in a heap in the dust.

I sprinted to Mirlande.

She dug her feet into the dirt and scrabbled away from me. "Who—"

"It's me," I said. "Marcus." I caught her easily, grabbed her under her arms and hauled her to her feet.

Her face was wide-eyed and dirt-streaked in the lantern's glow, her hair matted on one side of her head and flying away from the other. Seeing her own face staring back at her probably wasn't doing much to comfort her. I switched off my holohead.

"Marcus? But how—"

I reached behind her back and started working on her restraints. "We'll do storytime later. Right now, we need to move."

She struggled away from me. "Wait—"

I caught her arms. "Let's go. We've got to get—" But I noticed she wasn't looking at me.

I turned around. Three men stood behind the unconscious Tong, pointing their guns at us. They all wore holoheads. Two of them matched those worn by the pair of heavies I had just dispatched. The man in the center was short and lithe, with the glowing white face of a dragon skull.

TWENTY-EIGHT

The three men advanced toward us.

"Drop it," the thug on the right said.

I let my gun fall to the dirt.

He came forward and picked it up. Then he plucked the holohead unit off my shirt collar, removed my screen from my wrist and handed it all to the man with the dragon skull.

"Mr. Carver," Yuze Enriquez said. "I warned you to stay out of this."

He prodded the unconscious Tong with his foot, then kicked him when he didn't wake. That did the trick. The heavyset Tong moaned and raised a hand to the side of his head.

"Get up," Enriquez said.

The man got to one knee, pushed himself to his feet, wobbled slightly and held himself upright. Meanwhile, Enriquez's other henchman patted me down none too gently. When he saw the camera stuck to my temple, he peeled it off, held it up to Enriquez and crushed it in his meaty palm.

"Clever," Enriquez said. He jerked his head from the third henchman to Mirlande.

The Tong thug seized her shoulders and dragged her back to the center of the spotlight. She struggled, but her hands were bound behind her back, and he was twice her size. I doubt he even noticed. He kicked out her legs and sat her roughly on the ground. My shoulder ached where the Tong sniper had clipped me. I glanced down and saw specks of blood seeping through my shirt.

"And this." Enriquez inspected my holohead unit. "I haven't seen one of these yet. I'll have to try it sometime." He slipped it into his pocket.

The thug who had searched me stepped behind me and pinned my arms. Enriquez advanced, toying with his pistol. He stopped in front of me and grabbed my injured shoulder like a sadistic masseuse. I would have preferred he had just shot me again. I tried to twist away from his grasp, but the Tong behind me held me in place.

"Stop!" Mirlande yelled.

Enriquez squeezed harder. When I thought I might pass out from the pain, he released his grip, rocked back a step and hit me across the face with the muzzle of his gun, right to left and back again.

From somewhere deep inside me, I heard Julia yelling at me to move my head. I turned my face to absorb some of the first blow. I wasn't quick enough for the second strike, but the angle of my whip-lashed neck made it hard for him to get a clean shot. My knees buckled and the light-polluted night sky was suddenly full of stars, but the man behind me was kind enough to hold me upright.

Mirlande screamed something I couldn't make out through the ringing in my ears.

Enriquez waited until I managed to lift my head back up. "You don't listen very good," he said.

I spat blood and a pair of shattered teeth I hadn't really needed at his feet. This was shaping up to be a repeat of our last meeting, but I doubted he'd let me off with a warning this time. I said, "I listen just fine. But you obviously don't know me as well as you thought if you expected me to obey."

Enriquez laughed his cruel laugh, stepped around me and stood in front of Mirlande. She tried to rise, but the goon behind her planted a melon-sized hand on her shoulder and shoved her back into the dirt.

"You really fucked this up," I said.

"Did I?" He didn't bother to look at me.

Blood and saliva trickled down my chin. I bent my head and wiped my face against my shoulder. "You robbed Naomi Battle once. When Mirlande locked you out, you should have let it go."

"No, Mr. Carver. You should have let it go." He tapped his screen. "Maybe we're not that different. We both don't know when to stop. But I know how to win. That's why Ms. Battle is going to continue to pay me, and you are going to die."

I squinted at him against the glare of the lantern. With my head still throbbing, the light was brighter than a fusion reaction, but even a coffin two meters under would have been too bright. "That's your solution to every problem, isn't it? Just like the woman you murdered at Battle's place. Her name was Camila Giménez, by the way. What was she—collateral damage?"

He shrugged. "Call it leverage. And don't flatter yourself, Mr. Carver. You're no worse than a mosquito. I kill those too."

"Hello?" Battle's voice sounded from his screen.

"I have your man," Enriquez said.

"Who is this?" she asked.

"You know who it is. You can forget about Mr. Carver here."

Beyond the rim of the lantern light, the night was as silent and endless as the grave.

"Carver?" Battle said. "Who's that?"

"Don't get cute with me," Enriquez said. "Your man is as good as dead."

"I don't believe you."

Enriquez turned and aimed his screen at me, then back at Mirlande. "Your little rescue mission sped up the clock," he said. "Five a.m. You have less than six hours to save the girl."

"If you think you can steal from me, threaten me—"

"I do."

The empty black sky pressed down on us. A cold desert wind

kicked up and died as quickly as it had started.

"I'm going to find you." Battle's voice was low and menacing. "And when I do—"

Enriquez's laughter split the darkness. "You already found me. Look where that got you. You have the account number. Five a.m. tomorrow, or she dies."

He ended the call and flicked his gaze to the heavy holding me. "Kill him."

TWENTY-NINE

The goon pressed his gun against the base of my skull. The bite of steel against my skin was as cold as a Chicago winter morning.

"No!" Mirlande screamed. "Wait—"

I whistled, loud and sharp.

My would-be killer flinched. The pressure of the muzzle slipped ever so slightly off my neck. The other two thugs glanced at me and scanned their surroundings.

Enriquez hardly noticed. "He's bluffing," he said. "Shoot him."

The henchman's gun settled back against my neck. The metal had warmed to the temperature of my body. At the very least, I wouldn't die shivering.

Enriquez stood with his back to me, his hands in his pockets, staring out into the desert as if awaiting a call instead of the explosion that would mean my death. Mirlande sat with her head bowed and looked up at me with wide, glassy eyes. The thug guarding her gazed at the empty desert between us, apparently watching us both from the corners of his eyes. The recently revived man eyed me nonchalantly or woozily, the black eyes of his skull holohead as boundless and inevitable as the void.

Mirlande kicked at her guard's leg. From her position, seated on the ground with her hands restrained behind her, she couldn't put much force into the blow. Her foot caught the thug behind his knee. His leg wavered, but he remained standing. The henchman between us turned toward Mirlande. The gun eased off the back of my neck.

Most law enforcement and gun-owning citizens carried biometric lock weapons. If someone else got a hand on your gun, you didn't want them to be able to use it on you. But to thugs like the Tongs, guns were impersonal tools designed to be shared, used and discarded. And if the cops picked up a weapon with suspected criminal ties, a biometric lock meant a link to its owner. If experience was any guide, the Tongs would carry older model weapons without locking technology. Fortunately, I was right.

In the instant I felt the space between the gun and my neck, I shifted sideways, grabbed my guard's arm and threw him over my shoulder to the ground, wrestling the gun from his fingers as he fell. My shoulder liked that less than it had Enriquez's pincer grip. But my thug had scarcely hit the ground before I put a bullet through Mirlande's guard and then him, and aimed the pistol at the center of Enriquez's dragon skull holohead.

"Drop it," I said to the other Tong. He seemed unsure about whether to point his pistol at Mirlande or me. "Or I'll put the next one through both your boss's skulls." I jutted my chin at Enriquez. "You too. Put your weapons on the ground and slide them toward me."

Enriquez nodded at his heavy.

The other man hesitated.

"Do it!" Enriquez shouted.

They both set their pistols on the ground and kicked them in my direction.

I dropped to one knee without taking my gun off Enriquez, picked up their weapons and shoved them into the back of my waistband. "Now the screens," I said. "Ours and yours."

They threw those over too. I put mine back on and stuffed the rest into my pocket. I disarmed the dead Tongs as well.

"What next?" Enriquez tilted his head at Mirlande. "Cut her free?"

"No." I didn't want either of them anywhere near her. "Back away, both of you."

Enriquez and his thug took two steps back.

Tendrils of fire crawled from my right shoulder down my gun arm. My hand was going numb. "Get up, Mirlande."

It took her a minute to roll to one thigh, swing her other leg over, get to a knee and push herself to standing without using her hands.

"Come here."

She walked to my side. Her wide, unfocused eyes stared through my chest, and her hands trembled as I cut them free.

"It's all right," I whispered. "We're getting out of here."

She gave no sign of having heard me.

Enriquez stepped back into the center of the spotlight. "Where will you go, Mr. Carver?" His dragon holohead leered at me. "We're everywhere in this city. We see everything. There's nowhere for you to run. Nowhere for you to hide."

"Well, then," I said, "I guess you'd better give us a head start." And I put a bullet in both of their thighs.

We turned and ran. I had the Tong's screens, but I figured at least one of them had a neural link hidden under his holohead. It wouldn't be long before every Tong thug in the city was after us. I looked back to see Enriquez's remaining goon struggle to his feet and stagger after us, dragging his wounded leg. Then we were outside the holodisplay, and he disappeared behind us.

"You get all that?" I yelled.

"Yeah." Chaudhri's voice sounded from my screen. "Obviously, we lost the video when the Tongs found your camera. But the mike on your holo unit picked up everything. I'm sending it to Moreno now."

"Are you moving?" Battle asked. "I don't see you."

"Yeah," I said. "We're on our way."

"All right. We'll be there."

I aimed my screen's flashlight at the boulders a hundred meters ahead of us. "The other side of those rocks," I told Mirlande. "Come on."

She glanced behind us and ran beside me, her chest heaving and eyes focused on the boulders.

When we reached the rock formation, I guided Mirlande ahead of me, up and through the narrow cleft between the stones. Before I started to climb, I looked back once more. I saw nothing but dark and empty desert. Our pursuers were well behind us. By the time I pulled myself through the boulders and dropped to the ground on the other side, Battle's flyer was already descending a short distance ahead of us.

The tendons in Mirlande's long neck were rigid beneath her skin. "Naomi?"

I nodded. "That's our ride. Let's go."

I pulled Mirlande toward the flyer, but we had only taken a few steps before I heard a low, steady buzzing sound from the formation we had just traversed. Two black drones rose from the top of the rocks and darted in the direction of Battle's flyer. From each of the rock formations on either side, another drone lifted off and joined the attack.

"Go up!" I yelled.

The flyer was about to touch down when the canyon echoed with the crackle of gunfire. The flyer lurched and rose.

"Get out of here!" I said. "The Tongs have drones."

"I see them." Battle whipped the flyer into a sudden U-turn and sped toward the incoming drones. The nearest one slammed into her bumper and dropped like a swatted fly. The other three dodged past the flyer and spun back to give chase.

The sky ahead of us erupted with automatic fire. The flyer banked right. Chaudhri reached a pistol out the passenger window and returned fire. The drones veered after the flyer untouched and continued shooting. Chaudhri pulled his arm back inside. I heard the clang of bullets piercing the flyer's body. Battle pushed the flyer into a shallow dive, and the drones stuck with her.

"Go!" I yelled into my screen. Battle may have been an ex-fighter pilot, but a flyer was about as useful in a dogfight as a winged cargo ship. "You can't pick us up with those drones around, and we don't exactly have time to wait."

The flyer's engine whined as Battle pulled out of the dive and swerved to the left. The drones followed, still spraying bullets. Battle sent the flyer into as steep a climb as it could manage. "Keep shooting, Dev!" she said.

Distant gunshots rattled the night. The flyer's ascent rounded off, and the vehicle accelerated across the sky. The drones buzzed after it.

"Carver, get out of there," Battle said.

"I'm working on it."

"Now what?" Mirlande asked. Her gaze followed Battle's receding flyer.

"This way." I pulled her to my right. "Before those drones come back."

She stumbled, righted herself, and we took off running again.

"Can you make it?" Battle asked.

"We'll make it." In the distance, the Kwang accelerated with a rising whisper. "You've drawn the drones off."

"All right," Battle said. "Once I lose them, I'll circle back and find you."

Ahead of us, the Kwang surged around a pile of boulders and raced in our direction.

"Plan B," I said to Mirlande.

The car was closing rapidly, and Mirlande and I found one last burst of speed. The car skidded to a stop in front of us. We jumped in and took off, retracing the route I had taken with Moreno's CIs into the desert.

I ducked my head to look up through the window and saw the lights of Battle's flyer leaving the Tong drones behind. Ahead, the dull carbocrete shadow of the parking lot stood out against the lighter gray of the dusty landscape. Then the desert lit up around us. Roving white circles swept the sand, passed over the car, came back and settled on us. The Tongs were back.

I turned off the headlights and swerved the car away from the spotlights.

"Dev," I said, "we've got company."

"We're coming back," Battle said.

"Are they trying to hack us?"

"No signal yet," Chaudhri said. "If they try, your vehicle's standard security should hold up for a while. But I'm ready to step in if it looks like they're cracking it."

"That's the smart play." I dodged out of another spotlight. "Shut us down and take Mirlande alive. She's no good to them dead."

"Keep going," Chaudhri said. "I'll keep them busy."

We tore through the desert as the lights traced over our weaving vehicle. The way ahead of us was clear. To the east, there was nothing but a loose chain of opalescent streetlights strung across the darkness. But from the west, headlights raced in our direction. We slashed through the abandoned parking lot and swung out onto the road. The roving spotlights swept over us, lost us and found us again. The pair of headlights from the west bore down on us. I sped toward them.

"Are you crazy?" Mirlande screamed.

"That's a matter of perspective." I jammed my foot down as far as it would go.

The two cars ahead of us split in ninety-degree turns and stopped, blocking the entire road. I eased my foot off the pedal. When we were within shouting distance, I saw doors opening and two digital skulls gleaming like supernovas in the night. I saw rifles swinging around the doors. I ducked, pulled Mirlande down and accelerated. The pair of Tongs stood and swung their rifles in our direction, but it was too late. I swerved onto the right shoulder, then off the road, bumping and skidding past the two parked vehicles. The Kwang's front-left wheel lifted off the ground as we jerked back onto the road, and we hung there, tilting toward the shoulder, for what felt like an impossibly long time as I eased off the pedal and turned into the roll. Then the tire landed with a jolt, and I steered us down the highway.

In the rearview mirror, the two Tong vehicles righted themselves and continued their pursuit. Mirlande turned around the edge of her seat and looked behind us with an expression on her face that told me she saw them too. We had put some distance between us while the Tongs turned around, but the headlights expanding steadily in the mirror told me our lead wouldn't last long. I stomped on the accelerator, wondering even as I did so how I had survived so long with filament waste for brains. The Kwang surged up to the seventy-kilometer-per-hour limit and stayed there. I was used to driving police cars designed without the internal speed limit. I had never been on this end of a chase before, and it didn't look like my first experience would last very long.

THIRTY

The headlights behind us filled the entire rearview mirror.

"What are you doing?" Mirlande yelled. "Go—" She slumped back into her seat. "You can't."

"No," I said.

We sped into the night, between the looming shadow of the mountains and the yawning waste of the desert, as fast as we could go. It wasn't fast enough. One of the pursuing cars eased up behind us until we were nearly bumper to bumper. The other slid toward our left side. I swerved ahead of the car on our left and steered toward the center line of the road. The Tong car drifted wider and accelerated, pulling up beside me before I could cut him off. I jerked the wheel to the right, cleared the vehicle behind us and slammed on the brakes. The car on our left tried to follow us and almost collided with the rear Tong car. I sped up as much as I could, veering off the road and angling into the desert. The wheels spun momentarily in the dust, then caught solid ground and propelled us forward. Up ahead, a side street cut across our path. The Tong cars righted themselves and resumed their pursuit. The street was slightly elevated, and we bumped and rocked our way up the rise before making a sharp right onto the pavement. The Tongs followed, gaining steadily.

"We can't outrun them," Mirlande said.

"I know."

"Do you have a plan?"

I had the blind hope of a child and the clear-eyed sense of a cynic. "If we make it back to the city, Moreno can help us."

"LA? How far is that?"

"Thirty kilometers."

"Thirty kilometers! We can't hold them off that long."

"Where's your sense of adventure?" I handed her two of the non-biometric pistols I had taken off the Tongs. "Can you shoot?"

"No," she said. "I've never tried."

"It's easy," I said. "They're already loaded. Just aim and pull the trigger."

The Tongs had cozied up to our rear bumper again. Mirlande opened her window, twisted in her seat, reached her hand out and fired wildly behind us. The Tongs swerved to our left, cutting off her angle. She stretched her arm out and got off a few more errant shots before the slide locked open.

She settled back into her seat and examined the gun. "I think it's empty."

"It is." I scanned the road for an escape.

Mirlande set the dry pistol on the floor and reached the other weapon out the window.

"Wait," I said. "Until we really need it."

She drew her arm back in the car and gave a short, barking laugh. "It's going to get worse?"

As if in response, one Tong car crept up on our left side, while the other settled in directly behind us. The windows of the left-hand car slid down. A pair of blue-white skulls leered at me. Automatic rifles stabbed out beneath them.

Mirlande lunged across my lap.

"It's a little early for that." I struggled to keep control of the wheel with one good arm.

"Shut up." She scrambled over me and pressed herself against my window, her arms spread wide.

"What are you doing?" I shouted. "Get down!"

"You said they won't shoot me," she yelled back. "I'm no good to them dead. But they might try to shoot you."

"I was guessing! I wouldn't bet my life on it! Or yours."

"It's not yours to bet," Mirlande said.

There was no use arguing. We were both getting desperate.

The street ran along a rock wall on our left. I saw an opening ahead, tapped the brakes a few times to keep the Tongs behind us out of our trunk, then braked hard and veered left between the two cars and through the gap in the wall. I crashed through a barrier arm extending from a guardhouse and continued onto the tapering entry road to a gated community. The Tongs regrouped behind us, dodged the mangled barrier and resumed their pursuit. I took the first right, then a quick left, zigzagging through narrow, winding streets at forty kilometers an hour. Mirlande crawled back to her seat. We passed identical darkened houses whose black one-way windows shimmered like a calm night sea. I took every turn I saw, hoping to negate the Tongs' speed advantage. But every time I glanced in the mirror, the headlights reappeared, looming ever closer.

Sirens wailed from somewhere behind us and grew steadily louder. Soon, a pair of boxy, compact community security cars joined the pursuit, their flashing amber roof lights fractaled in the reflective windowpanes all around us. A salvo of gunfire rattled behind us. The security car on the right swerved off the road and smashed into a tree. The Tongs fired another burst. The front-left tire of the second security car exploded, and the car skidded and rolled onto its side.

Mirlande tore her gaze from the Tongs' vicious handiwork to me. "This is your plan B?"

I made a sharp right that almost sent us careening off the road. "Yeah."

"What's plan C?"

I didn't have time for second-guessing. I righted the car and accelerated into a lazy leftward curve. "I've got a platoon of hovertanks headed our way," I said. "Let me know when you see them, will you?"

We were nearing the opposite end of the gated community. The stone wall loomed behind the row of houses on our left. I took the next left, then another, and drove along the wall until I found the exit. We consigned another barrier arm to the recycling heap and made a quick left onto the outer road. The Tongs cleared the barrier wreckage and closed rapidly. They rode up behind us side-by-side and took turns plowing into one taillight and then the other, trying to send us into a spin. I veered left, right and left again. The Tongs followed, going wide to keep me from getting outside of them. When my rear bumper was clear, I slammed on the brakes and made a hard right turn. The Tongs shot past me, and I accelerated down another residential street. I made an immediate left before I could see the Tongs in my mirror, then another right, then left, right, left, right, snaking my way through the narrow streets.

Mirlande kneeled on her seat and stared out the rear window. "Did we lose them?"

"Maybe," I said. "For now." I spoke into my screen. "Dev. You there?"

"Yeah," he said. "Where are you?"

"Heading southwest toward the highway back to LA."

"Copy that," Battle said. "I think I see you."

"What about the two that were behind us?" I asked.

"Still there," she said. "Maybe a half a click away. They're a few streets back, so I don't think they can see you."

"Keep your distance for now. If they find us on the highway, we may need some cover."

We steered through a few more turns, then swung back onto the highway. I sped up as much as possible, but on the open road, without houses and trees streaming past us, it felt like we were moving in slow motion.

"You're clear," Chaudhri said. "The Tongs haven't followed you." Then, "Oh shit."

"What?" I asked.

"Two flyers incoming. Looks like the Tongs. I almost cracked their systems, but now they're back and they're headed in your direction."

"Reload, Dev," Battle said. "Get ready."

"Ready," he said. "The cars are turning your way," he added. "The flyers must have given them your location."

"How far to the city limit?" I asked.

"Twenty kilometers," Chaudhri said.

"Keep driving," Battle said. "We'll give you cover."

Suddenly, we were bathed in twin torrents of light as the two Tong flyers swept over us.

"Go!" Battle said. "We've got them."

The Tong flyers took up a position ahead of us. Battle sailed in from behind us, weaving from side to side. Gunfire shredded the sky. Battle charged, dipped, banked left, momentarily giving Chaudhri a clear shot at the Tong flyers' undersides. But the two vehicles split and ascended, dodging his fire. Battle roared past them and made a mid-air one-eighty no flyer was designed to make, then closed on the nearest one from behind.

Light flickered across my mirror, and I glanced at it to see the twin pairs of Tong headlights growing quickly. On our left, the wildfires loomed ever closer. Above, Battle hung doggedly on the tail of one Tong flyer, twisting and dodging as its occupants returned fire. The other flyer swung down from above them, and Chaudhri switched his aim back and forth, spraying bullets at each vehicle in turn.

Then I heard a grunt and Battle crying, "Dev!"

Their flyer went into a spin. Both Tongs bore down on them, raining automatic fire.

"Fuck!" Battle yelled. "Carver, I can't—"

Battle pulled out of the spin and darted left, right, left. But the flyer was falling steadily.

"Dev's been—" Alarms from inside the flyer drowned out her voice. "—he's gone."

Her rapid descent continued, but she somehow dodged the

Tongs' kill shots. Finally, the Tongs pulled up and circled back as Battle fell toward the mountain on our left.

"—sorry," she said.

"Naomi!" Mirlande screamed.

At the last moment, Battle pulled the flyer out of its freefall and directed it into a semi-controlled glide. It wasn't enough to stop her descent, but I hoped it would be enough to save her. She aimed the flyer down the slope, buying herself more time as the ground stretched away from her while her vehicle raced down to meet it. Beneath the incessant cabin alarms, I could hear her grunting as she struggled with the controls. She hit the trees mercifully east of the fires, and my screen howled with the terrific scraping, tearing roar of wood and metal smashing together. Then everything fell silent.

Mirlande stared out the rear window toward where her mentor and friend had gone down. "No," she said. "We have to—"

I didn't have to answer because the Tongs behind us had pulled up to our bumper, and there was no going back.

Some two hundred meters ahead, the Tong flyers descended and alighted in the road, blocking our way. We were right beneath the fires now. The wind was driving them away, leaving no smoke to obscure the noose tightening around our necks. The fires blazed orange and spectral in the cold night sky. Nothing lasts, but some things burn a little brighter before the end.

The two Tongs behind us nudged us forward. I jerked the Kwang from side to side, but they weren't falling for that maneuver again. I slowed as we closed to within a hundred meters, fifty meters, of the Tong flyers crouched in the road ahead. The cars behind us pushed us onward.

In front of the waiting flyers, a narrow road wound into the mountains. The Tong cars eased us forward once more, and I swung the wheel hard to the left and brought us out of the closing Tong trap and into the fires.

THIRTY-ONE

We crashed through a yellow-painted wooden barrier and headed up the mountain. The two Tong cars turned up the road behind us, then stopped. The flyers rose steadily above the treeline and soared overhead, their spotlights trained on us as I urged the Kwang onward as fast as it would allow me.

I looked at Mirlande sitting beside me. She pressed her full lips together and gave a single, tense nod.

We drove through another wooden barrier and into the forest. The shadows of tree limbs flickered over us under the Tong spotlights. Ahead of us, a tangerine glow suffused the backlit foliage.

I called Moreno.

"Are you clear?" he asked.

"Working on it," I said. "Have you been to the desert yet?"

"I'm here right now with the locals. Seems like there was a hell of a party. We've got five hosts, but only two of them are awake. One looks like our mutual friend."

"That's all of them. Although a few of their friends insisted on following us home."

The temperature was getting noticeably warmer. After playing stock racer for half an hour, I was already sweating by the time we pulled off the main road and headed up the mountain. Now my shirt was soaked through, and my clothes felt oppressive.

"Where are you now?" Moreno asked.

"That's why I called. There's been a slight change of plans. I need a new meeting point." I scanned the Kwang's onboard map, found where the road came out of the mountains into LA and gave Moreno the street names. "Somewhere near there. I'll let your guys pick the exact spot."

Moreno didn't answer for a moment. I checked my screen to make sure I was still getting a signal. Then he said, "Jesus, Carver. You are aware of the wildfire, right? The huge, bright orange, really hot thing that incinerates everything in its path?"

Ahead, the blackened husks of trees peeled past us one by one, like bandages torn off a raw, angry wound. If the Tong flyers were still above us, their spotlights were a drizzle on the sea of the inferno.

"Is that what I'm seeing?" I asked. "I suppose I'd better drive carefully."

"There has to be anoth—" Moreno cut out. "Carver! Car—"

The black shapes around us now were clouds of smoke instead of dead trees.

"Carver!—hear—I'll send—Don't—insane!"

The call ended. I confirmed the location on the LA side of the mountain and let the Kwang take over. Then we came around a bend, and the vermilion flush of scar tissue was gone, replaced by monstrous, gushing flames.

As far as I could tell, the Kwang was miraculously intact. I flicked all the window switches up, set the air to recirculate, turned off the climate systems and closed all the air vents. I wasn't taking any chances. If we started to roast, I would adjust accordingly. But if the dead air crept in, by the time we noticed we were suffocating, it would be too late.

We plunged into the flames. Mirlande drew a sharp intake of breath. Her cheeks were taut, her eyes wide with fear, and she leaned forward with her fingers splayed against the dashboard, as if trying to push the car through the inferno. The Kwang's display lit up with warnings: temperature, air quality, visibility. I cleared them all and made sure the car stayed on course.

"We're never going to make it," Mirlande said.

"We weren't going to make it on the road," I replied.

"I know."

The Tongs had cut off our safest escape path on the highway below. I could only hope the fire hadn't done the same to our alternate route. If we could keep moving, we had a chance. In that respect, the Kwang's compressed air engine actually worked in our favor. I had used up most of the air tank following Battle and Chaudhri to the three potential kidnapping sites. But the heat from the fire would increase the air pressure and extend our range. As long as the temperature didn't spike too quickly, the tank's relief valve would let off excess pressure to prevent an explosion. But if the flames or smoke or a fallen tree made the road impassable, I would turn us around and hope the way behind us was still clear and the Tongs had given up and gone home. If we got trapped, I'd open up the vents and see if we could fall asleep before the flames ate us alive.

I couldn't see beyond a few meters in any direction. The fire was everywhere. In the gaps between flames, clouds of black smoke swirled about, the dark and the light churning like partners in a macabre dance. The surrounding air crackled and popped as the fire pounced upon stray leaves and twigs and tore them to shreds. Great roaring sounds signified exploding tree trunks and were accompanied by sudden gusting air currents that rocked the car.

The Kwang wove around a fallen tree that blocked most of the road. The heat inside the car was becoming unbearable. I was swimming in my clothes. My brain sloshed about inside my skull. My shoulder throbbed, my jaw ached, and my vision danced. I struggled to breathe the thick, scorching air against my bruised ribcage.

"Look," Mirlande said.

I saw nothing but blurry, wavering fire. Next to me, sweat poured down Mirlande's face. Her hands were still pressed against the dashboard, and she was leaning forward with a delirious intensity as the reflected inferno sparkled in her dark eyes.

"It's beautiful," she whispered.

I followed her gaze. The fires swirled and plunged like a thousand tropical birds in flight. The air roared like tidal waves crashing against the shore, and the black smoke rolled in behind it all like the close of starless night. It was beautiful—in a terrifying way. But then everything beautiful is terrifying. I closed my eyes. The fire painted itself against my eyelids. I wondered if I would actually feel my brain melt. We were trapped in our feeble bodies in a tiny shell of metal and glass, careening through a power capricious and untamable. Inside our shell, the world was sweltering, stifling. But outside, everything was wild and free and pure. My hand reached for the air vents. Mirlande pressed herself forward, almost rising out of her seat, the fire glowing in her eyes.

The Kwang's display caught my eye. The screen was flickering in and out as the software struggled to reach the satellite feed. But our little arrow was advancing, skipping upward as the screen blinked off and on. I pulled my hand back. I stared into the flames. Suddenly, they parted, if only for a second, and beyond them I glimpsed a dark tapestry in shades of deep green, blue and brown, studded with millions of gemstones—the lights of the city below. The curtains of flame closed, then opened again. I watched the arrow on the screen flit upward with fewer interruptions.

"Carver ... Carver ..."

Mirlande gazed out the window at the withering flames, her lips slightly parted in what looked like numb disbelief.

"Carver ... are you there?"

"Hello?"

"Carver, damn it, where are you?" It was Moreno.

I worked my tongue free of the stultifying jungle of my mouth and gave him our approximate location.

"Are you okay?"

"Yes," I said. "I think so."

Suddenly, the entire city opened up below us. The fires receded to our right and behind us, the vanguard flames steadily devouring the northwest edge of the city.

"Do you have the address?" Moreno asked.

"No. Tell me again."

He did. "God, you're a crazy motherfucker. Now get out of that car and go somewhere safe."

Moreno and I had worked out an escape plan in case things got bad, which was the understatement of the century. All Mirlande and I had to do was make it to the meeting location and stay out of the Tongs' sight for five minutes before we arrived. There were no spotlights overhead, so we were okay there. Moreno had pulled five cars from impound and found eight cops he could trust enough to join his sting operation without telling anyone else what they were doing. One car was meant for Mirlande and me. Each of the other four would have a pair of Moreno's cops—one driving, one in the front passenger seat. We would all wear holoheads, each of them different.

Moreno had instructed his four cars where to go: San Pedro, Dana Point, Mojave, Ventura. "Where you go is up to you," he told me. "I don't want to know. I don't want any of my people to know. You get there, and you get safe."

We continued down the mountain, past the blackened carcasses of trees and the smoldering ruins of homes. Stray embers drifted on the swirling winds. But the bulk of the fire had moved on in search of fresh fuel. The meeting location was under a grove of fern pines along a side road in the foothills. The Kwang was on its last puffs of air when we pulled under cover. One cop stood among the five cars. The others waited in the vehicles as we exited the Kwang.

"You Carver?" The lead cop stared beyond us with a look that said he was no longer sure about what he'd gotten himself into.

"Yeah." I followed his gaze. Even in the dim light from the nighttime city below, I could see the Kwang's cracking, blistered paint and the melted, worn tread of the tires.

The cop regained his businesslike persona and pointed at an empty vehicle. "That's you." He hesitated, probably mulling whether to ask if we knew what we were doing, then turned and headed for his own car.

Mirlande and I got in and switched on our holoheads as spotlights swept over the tree canopy. I let the four other cars leave first. The spotlights followed. Then I pulled out and eased down toward the city. I directed the car toward Glendale and instructed it to find a route that was heavily trafficked but still moving. No gridlocks, no empty roads. After a few kilometers, we picked up the freeway heading southeast. The smoke rolled down the mountain behind us and swooped southwest across the city. The fire evacuation was in full swing, and we immersed ourselves in the steadily flowing tide of vehicles. In Glendale, I parked in a covered garage at a jumper depot, where we crammed into a packed car for a brief flight south across downtown. There, we walked two blocks to the maglev station and boarded a train for San Diego. Even in the middle of the night, our compartment was half full, all of us fleeing from something. We were about halfway down the coast when Moreno called.

"I've got good news and bad news," he said. "Good news: the Tongs followed three of my cars. Eventually, my guys confronted them. Even if I didn't trust those six, no cop wants to be chased. They arrested five Tongs. Combined with the five you took care of in Agua Dulce, we've dealt the Tongs a pretty good blow."

"What's the bad news?"

Moreno sighed. "We didn't get Enriquez. We scanned all the Tongs' prints. The guy who wore the dragon skull holo is John Zhao. It could be an alias. I don't know. We're still trying to work everything out. But I think it's best to assume Enriquez is still out there and still in charge."

"And you think he'll come after us."

"From what we know about Enriquez, he's utterly ruthless and he hates to lose. My guess is he won't stop chasing you until someone makes him. So wherever you are now, keep going."

"How far?" I asked.

"As far as you can. The Tongs have connections in Latin America, China, Russia, probably parts of Europe. There's a rumor that one of Enriquez's lovers ran off with another guy a few years back. The Tongs found them in Macau. Enriquez had them brought back to LA. He tortured the man to death while the woman watched. Then he let his men have their way with her before he killed her."

I looked at Mirlande. She was a stranger in her holohead, a middle-aged Asian woman with short, straight hair and eyelids heavy with exhaustion. But her jaw was set, and there was a hint of the fire I had seen in her gaze as we navigated the inferno.

"All right." I ran a hand over my throbbing jaw. "I'm leaving you with a pretty big mess on your hands."

"You are," Moreno said. "But sometimes that's the best way to start making things clean again."

Mirlande's screen lit up as soon as I ended the call. Her face followed suit. "Naomi."

"Are you safe?" Battle's voice sounded exhausted but resolute.

"Yes." Mirlande's voice trembled. "Are you?"

"I'm fine. I'll be fine."

"And Dev?"

I could hear Battle's strained breathing through Mirlande's screen. "He didn't make it."

Mirlande's hand went to her mouth, and she uttered a single choked sob.

"I know," Battle said. "But he would be happy if he knew you were okay. Is Carver with you?"

"I'm here."

"Get her somewhere secure," Battle said. "Your money is already in your account—plus enough to get you anywhere you need to go. I'm going to destroy these assholes, but it won't happen overnight. I'll let you know when it's safe to come back."

"Naomi," Mirlande said. "I'm so sorry. I—"

"It's okay," Battle replied. "I'm sorry I didn't earn your trust. Now go."

The train whipped along the darkened coast, its faint lights skimming over the lapping black waves. I had an idea where we could go, but for a moment, it was enough to feel the past racing away from us as we plunged into the night's embrace.Mirlande fell asleep and was soon leaning against me, her head resting on my shoulder, her breath coming in regular, gentle murmurs. I watched her for a minute, then went back to scanning satellite imagery on my screen's display until I saw what I was searching for. You can find almost anything in the world today, as long as you have an idea of where to look.

Twenty minutes later, we were in San Diego. I picked up a delivery of bandages, antibiotics and new clothes at the station and patched up my bloody shoulder as best I could. Then I kept us moving, staying in crowds when possible, changing our holoheads frequently. We boarded an airtran headed south, and I bought us a pair of fake passports from an old contact in Chicago. We landed in Tijuana, just outside the airport. From there, we caught a flight to Mexico City, then boarded another airliner to Sydney as soon as our feet touched the ground.

I sank into my seat, the last traces of adrenaline crept back out of my bloodstream, and I fell into a dreamless sleep. I awoke somewhere over the Pacific.

Mirlande was gazing out her window. When I shifted in my seat, she said, "You're welcome, by the way."

"For what?" I asked.

She turned toward me and beamed. It was the first time I had seen a genuine smile on her face, and it was obscured by her digital mask. I imagined it was as beautiful and terrifying as the wildfires.

"For saving your life," she said. "Who tripped her guard in the desert so that your guard was distracted? Who was your human shield as we drove away in a speed-limited car?"

"You're right." I laughed. "Thank you."

She reached up and put her hand on my jaw. "Does it hurt?"

"Yes," I said. "But not as bad as it did before."

She held my gaze. "I know what you're doing. You can't stay with me."

I didn't answer. Some beauty is terrifying because of its power, some because of its transience.

"Do you know where we're going?" she asked.

I told her.

"I like that," she said. "I can stay there. For a little while, at least."

From Sydney, we continued on to Perth, and it was only because our next flight wasn't until the following day that I decided we could stop running for a few hours. We found a room in the airport hotel, and when I finally deadbolted the door to our room, I allowed myself to believe we had left the Tongs behind us. When I turned away from the door, Mirlande was waiting for me, her holohead extinguished and her face bare. I kissed her, firm and full on the lips. And for a moment, the whirlwind pace of the past twenty-four hours slowed to a halt, and time stood still as our lips locked and our chests rose and fell together with the deep breaths of relief. Then her hands were on my back, while mine were tugging off her shirt, and we were drawing each other toward the bed, the world accelerating once more as we fell against each other into the waiting sheets.

THIRTY-TWO

The island should not have existed. I had read it was once one of twenty-seven in an atoll, arranged in a circle like a string of pearls in the Indian Ocean. Of the other twenty-six, only one still rose above sea level, the scant construction that had been there now destroyed by or abandoned to the sea. Our destination occupied the southwest curve of the atoll, and the reefs and shoals that remained of the other islands still shielded it from the westward currents. In addition, the Australian government considered this six-square-kilometer patch of sand an important military outpost and, with the help of some anonymous private investor, they had preserved every grain they could.

We descended over dense palm forests and pristine white beaches, only a few of which gave access to the clear, turquoise waters. The Australians had dredged the surrounding seabed and deposited the mineral along the shore to raise the land up. Concave seawalls guarded the shorelines, ready to throw back any waves that would threaten the surviving island paradise. Looking down at what remained of the atoll, I understood why a group of moralizing California legislators had passed their combustion law. I didn't love the way it was written, even though that design helped pay my bills. But it also turned once-peaceable citizens against each other and gave people like William Schuyler the ammunition that had sent me running halfway around the world.

We walked off the airliner, across the tarmac and through the squat, square pavilion that functioned as the airport. Then we continued on foot along a road that followed the crescent curve of the island. The land was so flat and narrow that we could see the ocean on both sides. It was hot, with the sun slipping in and out of the foamy white clouds and the occasional solitary palm tree offering little cover. But there was a breeze blowing off the water from our right, we each carried nothing but a pack with basic toiletries and a few spare clothes, and after days of running, it was a relief to stroll along a quiet road in one of the last sparsely inhabited tropical refuges on Earth. We passed a few single-story rectangular buildings with low peaked roofs and driveways leading toward the coasts and modest homes shaped like many-sided polygons raised on stilts. The occasional car trundled past us. But for the most part, we were alone with each other, surrounded by rustling green leaves and the placid murmur of the ocean under an immaculate azure sky.

After about thirty minutes, we came to a low pyramidal roof, supported by bamboo pillars at each corner and open on all sides. A sign hanging off the roof read "Island Boats," and a double outrigger with a raised mast but no sail rested in the grass out front. The hull and outriggers were made of some kind of polymer with pale blue, green and white marbling that suggested a swirling ocean tide. We turned off the road and approached the shop. The back of the shelter led to a beach on the island's shielded eastern bay. A pair of similarly marbled outriggers sat on the sand, their sails furled. Inside, a man was bent over another upturned hull. The craft was about six meters long, resting on a crude wooden rack, and he was going over it centimeter by centimeter with a battery-powered hand polisher.

He glanced up when we stepped into the shade. "How can I help you?"

"Hello, Mr. Schuyler," I said.

He continued his work while looking us over from under his hat brim. But the polisher never stopped moving. His free hand slid along the hull ahead of it, feeling for imperfections with the easy dexterity that belied a lifetime of experience. Then he crouched in a way that made my knees ache and stared along the keel. He stood and walked toward us, one hand tracing the surface of the hull, then turned his back and bent over the boat once more.

"How did you find me?" His voice just rose over the drone of the polisher.

"The portrait in your sitting room," I said. "Cherrier told me the story."

Ellory Schuyler crept away from us, never lifting his head from his work. Beyond him, metal molds of hulls rested on racks with clamps hanging off the ends. In the back was a long, flat contraption with a hinged top that looked like an oversized sandwich press. On either side of that, cloth sacks rested on the sand, each of them overflowing with plastic debris.

Schuyler said, "If you've come to take me back—"

"I haven't," I said. "I have news about your son."

The polisher stopped. Schuyler straightened and turned to face us. "All right." He gestured to a set of wooden chairs at the back of the shop, facing the ocean. "Let's sit."

I told him the entire story, from William and Battle to Mirlande, King, Camila, Eindhoven and the Tongs. Schuyler listened quietly. In his face, I could see aspects of the holohead William had worn, but the elder Schuyler's features were sharper, all hard lines with no softness or polish, like an artist's unfinished portrait. He had a high forehead and a long, angular nose with thin, colorless, cracked lips and hollow cheeks stubbled gray and white. He wore a loose shirt opened to his collarbones and rolled up his sinewy forearms. Most of all, I recognized his slitted green eyes, which sparkled like the ocean laid out before us. When I told him why William had hired me, his jaw hardened, and one side of his mouth parted in a bitter sneer. When I got to William's death, his eyes went blank and his features slackened, the taut, lined skin of his cheeks and forehead sagging like melting suet.

"You shouldn't have had to hear about this from me," I said, "but you deserve to know before anyone else."

He nodded and stared out at the gently rolling surf.

"I'm sorry." Mirlande reached out and touched his wrinkled, sun-spotted hand. "I'm sure Naomi would feel the same if she knew."

He continued to watch the waves in silence. A solitary gull darted over the beach, banking back and forth before alighting on the roof behind us.

"These islands didn't have filter bots until a few years ago." Schuyler inclined his head toward the sea. "And these shores had more accumulated plastic pollution than almost any place on Earth. How long have we had those bots along every few kilometers of coast in the States? Two decades?" He gestured at the marbled polymer boats on the beach. "Made from plastic debris found on the beaches of this island. We collect it, sort it, melt it down and mold it into the hulls. So I understand the sentiment behind environmental laws. But the way they wrote the California bill—it wasn't about protecting the environment. Not really. You ask me, it was their way of getting back at Texas and the other states for that civil abortion law. But they didn't think about the effect it would have on the millions of people who don't make the laws but have to live among neighbors incentivized to spy on them."

His eyes lingered on his completed boats for a moment before drifting back out to sea. "I wasn't a good father," he said. "I never had any illusions about that. There was one thing I was good at, and I did it." The left side of his mouth curled back in a bitter half-smile. "Maybe I hoped William would follow my example. Find something he loved and excelled at and pursue that goal with every breath he took. But even that is giving myself too much credit." He lifted his cap and ran a hand through his thinning white hair. "I wanted to build, but I didn't want to do it there, surrounded by the sycophants, the hangers-on, the so-called cooperators. So when Isabel passed ..." He fell silent and wiped his thumb and forefinger over his eyelids and down his face.

Then he shook his head, and his face resumed its aristocratic tension. "But you didn't travel halfway around the world to tell me about William."

"No," I said. "I have a favor to ask." I finished the story, telling him about the Tongs kidnapping Mirlande and how we'd escaped. "There aren't many places in the world to hide these days. But you've found one."

He glanced at Mirlande. "So now you want me to hide you too."

"We don't want you to do anything you haven't been doing this past year," I said. "You've found the perfect hiding place. We're just asking you to share it."

"And if I refuse, you'll expose my secret to the world?"

"I don't think it will come to that."

"No," Schuyler said. "It won't." He looked at Mirlande again. "So you worked for Naomi?"

"Yes," she said.

He nodded curtly. "That's enough of a resume for me. You're hired."

"As what?"

"You were Naomi's chief of staff. I could use someone to be the face of this place. Someone who knows how things work and can relate to people."

"All right."

"I doubt I can pay you what Naomi did. But I can find you a place to live and make sure you have enough money to get what you need." He stood and extended his hand to Mirlande.

She reached up and shook it. "Deal."

Schuyler turned to me. "What about you? You don't strike me as the island type. But I'm sure I could find a role for you."

"He's not," Mirlande said. "He hates vacations."

I recalled our conversation in the hallway of Battle's home office space. It felt like a lifetime ago. "The Tongs want her," I said. "She's the one who got away. And the DA will need someone to take the stand if this thing goes to court."

"Well, you look like you can take care of yourself," Schuyler said.

I shrugged. "Some days I do better than others."

I stood. Mirlande looked up at me and forced a smile. Her eyes told me it was a lie. But we had worked things out in advance.

"Don't say goodbye," she had told me. "I said goodbye to both my parents, and I never saw them again."

"Naomi said she's going to bury the Tongs," I said. "But it won't happen right away."

She gave me a wry half-grin. "I wouldn't want to be them. If Naomi wants something, she gets it."

"I wouldn't either," I said. "I'll let you know when it's safe to come back."

She nodded. "When you leave me, don't look back. Just walk away as though you were coming back tomorrow."

I told her I would do just that.

A few days earlier, we had sat in her car on the edge of a mountain, staring into the night, and I had worked my way back to the truth while the events that started with King, William Schuyler and Mirlande were spinning forward, throwing off fresh, deadly consequences. Now our orbits had reversed, and I was moving forward, while she was forced to live in the past.

When I walked out of Schuyler's boat shop, the sun was spreading its last golden rays over the western shore as the Earth turned away from it. I never looked back, but I was conscious when the road curved around a palm grove that the shop would no longer be visible behind me. I had never wanted to go to space, but I understood why a man like Ellory Schuyler would want to turn his back on the ugly, crooked, spiteful world we had come from. But that was my world. I wasn't going to fix it. But I was going to be there, water bucket in hand, when the cleansing fires finally burned it all down. I had an hour to catch the return flight to Perth, and I walked alone, back down the empty island road that would eventually lead me home, while the clear island sky bloomed orange and lavender until the sun dipped below the horizon.

Meet Carver's police officer grandfather in Greg Hickey's crime novel *Parabellum*. Four high-achievers battling psychological demons. Any of them might snap. But which one will become a killer? **Visit mybook.to/mirpbp or scan the QR code below to read *Parabellum* and find out.**

* * *

Download Carver's Chicago Police Department personnel file when you sign up for Greg Hickey's newsletter at **greghickeywrites.com/retrograde-reader**.

* * *

Want to help a fellow reader? Reviews are essential in leading other readers to their new favorite book, and you can help them by writing a few sentences about *Murder in Retrograde*. It doesn't have to be a detailed analysis, just your honest opinion about what you liked about the book and who you think might enjoy it.

Visit greghickeywrites.com/retrograde-review to share your thoughts.

ABOUT THE AUTHOR

Greg Hickey is a former international professional baseball player and forensic scientist and current endurance athlete and Amazon bestselling author. His previous works include the novels *Parabellum* and *Our Dried Voices*, the latter of which was a finalist for *Foreword Reviews'* INDIES Science Fiction Book of the Year Award. He lives in Chicago with his wife and daughter.

Connect with Greg at greghickeywrites.com.

ACKNOWLEDGEMENTS

This book would not have been possible without generous contributions from the following people.

Mark Fyers, Milan Djordjevic, Darryl Perry, Larry Roy and Sandra Webb Smith read early drafts of this novel and offered insightful feedback on genre conventions, character development, plot holes, story pacing and more. Jason Allen-Forrest, Nilesh Makan and Julie Barrett provided last-minute suggestions. As always, my wife and meticulous proofreader Lindsay Simpson scoured the penultimate draft of this manuscript for any lingering errors.

Murder in Retrograde is a far better book thanks to their time and input.